Graham & Swaggart Publishing
wgac@att.net

Names: Wellborne, Connie | Santana, Cherry
Title: Suzze Osmond Ex-Christian, Move Over Jesus There's a New Girl in Town, Episodes 1-2
Summary: Televangelist Suzze Osmond has fallen from grace and seeks to redeem herself.
Identifiers: ISBN 978-0692673522 (paper) | ASIN: B06XCL7GM8 (epub)
Subjects: Satire | Fiction | Religion | Atheism | Religious War

www.SuzzeOsmond.com

Printed in the United States of America

To Shirley, Mentor and Contributor

-- And --

To the memory of Christopher Hitchens,

a single voice among many

but the most exuberant voice of all.

 са

What is hateful to you, do not do to your fellow man.

Hillel the Elder (c 110 BCE - 10 CE)

As it will be in the future, it was at the birth of Man,

There are only four things certain since Social Progress began.

That the Dog returns to his Vomit,

And the Sow returns to her Mire,

The Whore to her Bed,

And the burnt Fool's bandaged finger goes wabbling

back to the Fire.

Rudyard Kipling, from Proverbs 26:11

Welcome to the War Between the Christians and the Atheists

Artful, cynical, good fun

Entertaining, **thought-provoking,** captivating and mystical

ferociously profane

... many an **imaginative, surprising** scene and plot point

... **zippy dialog and a fast-paced narrative in a complex, layered plot** ...

... **satirical** view of religion, politics and life.

Surreal, metaphysical, bizarre, irreverent and **oddly poetic**

Reads like a TV series

Could this silly bit of fluff and puff, this slap-stick comedy serve up and address real moral and ethical questions and then honestly and cleverly answer them? ... hints of Voltaire and Vidal, Tom Robbins and Tom Wolfe.

Love the humor, love the cleverness, love the developing story, **love the War on Christianity theme ...**

Connie Wellborne *&* Cherry Santana
Present

Suzze Osmond
Christian

starring in

Move Over Jesus, There's a New Girl in Town

Episodes 1 2

Episode 1 Gotta Go

Scenes

| Gotta Go

SUZZE OSMOND PAUSED TO EXAMINE the scratches her broken fingernails were making in the soft leather of the Barcalounger she was dragging to the curb.

She stuck her index finger in her mouth, chewed off the offending burr, rolled it across her tongue, and spit it out.

Back to work.

Two steps and slide.

Two steps and slide.

She backed the recliner down the hill, her bare feet biting into the faux cobblestones of her textured driveway, which emptied into Buttermilk Road, which, in turn, wound and curved past dozens of other driveways just like hers in this most exclusive of exclusive neighborhoods on the south end of Aspen, Colorado.

Two steps and slide.

Two steps and slide.

Halfway there, she paused again to look down at the hundred or so people on the other side of the wrought iron security gate who edged forward when they saw her reappear.

Two steps and slide.

Two steps and slide.

The chair was heavy.

She was tired.

She repeated the cadence in her head, two steps and slide,

two steps and slide, until she reached the bottom of the hill.

She stopped a few feet short of the gate to catch her breath, closing her eyes and resting her head against the back of the chair, letting her fingers trace the ridges and scrolls of a logo, her logo, a big, ornate S, all swirls and twirls and curlicues in blue and pink and lavender embroidered into the cream-colored leather.

A few seconds later, as if on cue, a slow crescendo began to arise from the other side, *Sooz-zee, Sooz-zee, Sooz-zee.*

Suzze opened her eyes, raised her head and looked over the crowd.

"Hey Suzze Woozy," someone called out as she punched in the security code.

"Cutie Pootie," another one chimed in.

The price of fame.

Word was out.

There was shit to be had.

But unlike the piles of junk in front of the foreclosures all over town, this was coming out in dribs and drabs, one piece at a time.

Mostly it was good stuff. High dollar stuff.

The Aspen Times, resorting to sensational headlines to prop up their declining circulation, blasted 'Who The F**k Throws Away A Bentley!' across the top of Page One in 120 point sans serif extra-bold. Nice car. On the curb. Keys in the ignition. Gone in 60 seconds.

But as valuable as most of the stuff was, the crowd camped outside the gate and spilling onto the road were there as much for the entertainment as they were for the booty. It was a picnic. A party. A family affair. Simple insanity played out in real time for the world to see.

Indie journalists from around the world sat in front of green screens pretending to be live and on the scene, spouting social commentary in a dozen different languages.

Local television chose the most derelict from the crowd for the 6 o'clock news, encouraging each one to hold up his or her favorite piece of Suzze memorabilia, a treasure to be sure.

'Suzze Takes A Dump' along with a hundred tasteless variations headlined a hundred different blogs, each trying to create the most controversy over America's newest celebrity refugee. Controversy meant page views. Page views meant ads. Ads meant money, maybe only a penny a pop but it was a living for the stuck-at-homes – sort of.

Suzze had gone viral.

Trending again.

Tweeted back to life after a mysterious absence during which she was reported to have had a near-death experience.

As with every tragedy, Internet marketing opportunities were born.

There was a box of camels. Stuffed camels. Porcelain camels. Squeaky camel toys. Cute little camel keychains. One hump. Two humps. Hundreds of them. No Kewpie dolls. No Teddy bears. No Beanie Babies. Just camels. A fat guy with greasy hair snatched them up and advertised them on Craigslist, each with its very own Certificate of Authenticity which he downloaded from a clip art site. The way he figured it, he could pay off his credit cards. Or not.

But wait, there's more.

A sixteen-year-old girl living with her unemployed family in a flophouse motel outside of Orlando started selling embroidered Suzze bathrobes, pointing that the sash must be missing for the robe to be genuine, which hers, and only hers, were. She registered the name suzzewear.com and had her website up and running the same day. The girl, Sarah Gonzales was her name, hooked up with a guy in India named Patel to source the goods and embroider the breast pocket logo. $39.95 a pop. Three easy payments. Another global business born, everything outsourced and offshored. The girl made $11.57 on every transaction direct to her PayPal account, running it all from a computer at the public library. Zero investment. Zero overhead. *Damn, why didn't I think of that? a million jealous people whined.*

Then there were the Thomas Kinkade paintings, dozens of them tossed in a pile on the curb outside the gate. At first, no one wanted them, didn't know what they were. A couple of desperate housewives rifled through them and ripped the canvases out of eight of the frames to make placemats like they saw on the Katie Brown Workshop. Finally, someone Googled thomas + kinkade and figured out the paintings were actually worth something, which caused a fist fight and even more broken frames and ripped canvases. Those that survived appeared on eBay a few hours later. *Jackpot!*

With the publicity came the publicity seekers.

Starting with TMZ. The stuff didn't matter to them. All they wanted was a picture of her pussy. Correspondents on site. Stay tuned. Only a matter of time.

Of course, there was a mime. Of course, he wore a bathrobe with no sash. Of course, he wore a frizzy blond wig and fake boobs. He swished and swirled and pretended to drag imaginary furniture and shove it out of an imaginary gate, pretending to pepper spray anyone who pretended to get too close. When the audience grew bored with that he sat on an imaginary toilet and made funny faces.

No doubt, it was the juggler the crowd liked best, especially the kids. Frying pans, pepper grinders, whips, paddles, dog collars, he could juggle it all, five at a time.

A bible thumping preacher, shirt sweated wet, alcohol on his breath, summoned fire and brimstone down upon them all until someone flicked a Wüsthof paring knife dead center in the 'o' of his Holy Bible. Incensed, the preacher pounded his fist higher still, calling for the wrath of God to avenge the injustice. A kid pulled a pink Taser from his pillowcase full of Suzze collectibles, shot the preacher in the ass and turned up the juice as they all watched him slobber and jitterbug on the ground.

When the preacher came to, he stumbled down the road, the wires still pinned to his rear end, the Taser bouncing along behind like a tin can tied to a dog's tail.

"Oh my God, Oh my God, Oh my God," he moaned.

The kid who shot him cupped his hands and yelled, "Hey asshole. That's OMG, OMG, OMG."

"LOL," his buddy hollered after him.

As they laughed and jeered, an old man sitting cross-legged on the ground in the middle of the bunch reached over, pulled the knife from the bible and put both under his raincoat, unnoticed by anyone.

Suzze was used to crowds, knew how to play them.

She smiled along with the self-righteous women who felt sorry for her matted hair and humiliation and nodded to the sad old men who dreamed of getting her into the rack.

The teenage boys were the most annoying of all, snapping away with their iPhones and assorted digital devices. Her clinically perfect breasts had already been splashed across the blogosphere. Good money, but not great money. They were after bigger game, a high def jpeg of Suzze's Velcro. It was rumored that her vajayjay was vajazzled, with Christ himself dangling from her Holy of Holies. All they had to do was get to it before TMZ. One of them, sensing an opportunity about to be lost and willing to risk electrocution poked his arm through the rungs of the iron gate and between her legs with the camera resting upward in his palm.

Click. He had it.

But as he lay on his back examining his catch in the preview screen, all he saw was a dark blur with a glint of gold in the middle. Worth a try. Maybe he could Photoshop it.

Suzze Osmond had lived all of her adult life in front of cameras and learned long ago how to show what she wanted to show and how not to show what she did not want them to see. *Sorry boys, no crotch shots today.*

Time to get on with it.

It was a routine that had taken some practice. She slipped on her electrician's gloves, grabbed the back of the recliner and swung it around, then cracked the electrified gate just enough to squeeze the chair through, grunted and gave it one last shove before snapping the gate shut again, as she had been doing, box by box, piece by piece, for almost a week.

Early on, a few unhinged souls had in mind to charge the gate those few seconds after it was opened, when Suzze still had her hands full. She gave the first two or three rows an introductory pepper spray until they realized there was no need to steal the shit when the shit comes to you. They behaved after that.

Suzze looked them over, her uninvited yard party. She wouldn't miss them. Not a single one.

She slipped off the heavy rubber gloves and re-entered the security code.

That was it.

The last piece.

No more chairs.

No more cars.

No more appliances.

No more shoes, evening gowns, designer cookware, artwork, flatscreens, memorabilia, or bric-a-brac.

Nothing left.

Over.

Done.

Mission accomplished.

As Suzze stood there congratulating herself, a ragged woman jumped up, plopped down in the recliner, crossed her arms and leaned back, smiling, claiming it as her own.

Just as quickly, two burly Mexicans lifted the chair with her in it onto the back of a rusted out F-150 Longbed. The woman was grinning ear to ear with her arms still crossed in defiance when the biggest of the two grabbed her by the scruff of the neck, yanked her off the truck and through the air, tossing her back onto the pavement where she had been sitting just a minute before.

Suzze watched from the other side of the gate as the chair on the back of the truck wound down the road, around the curve and over the hill, her logo fading out of sight.

As it disappeared, forever she thought, she felt a queasiness deep in her belly, an urgent, loose, liquid softness.

It was a long trot back up the hill.

She hoped she could make it in time.

| deAngelo

ON THE SAME DAY, Sunday, at about the same time, 3 p.m. that Suzze was trotting back up the hill, deAngelo Freeman was running for his life.

At least that's the way he thought about it whenever he had possession. He possessed the football. The football possessed him. They were one and the same.

A lot had happened in the last three seconds. He had caught the ball deep in the end zone and was crossing the twenty-yard line.

The game clock had run out.

He was down five and a touchdown would win the game.

Eighty yards to go.

Eleven big men trying to stop him from getting there.

deAngelo froze. In his mind, he froze the action around him, something he couldn't explain but to him it seemed as if he were stopping time itself.

He spotted the defense and their positions on the field like players on a chess board.

He saw the path through the obstacles already overcome.

It was surely a gift from his Lord and Savior Jesus Christ, this supernatural talent that it seemed only he possessed.

After a split, split second, he turned everything back on and started running again, having never paused for an instant as far as 90,000 people in Sun Life Stadium could see.

The multitudes ran right alongside him, just a foot away, or so it seemed as they watched him on the video boards high above the stadium.

Millions more watched from high-def plasmas in homes and bars across America.

And when deAngelo scored the winning touchdown, game over, just twelve seconds later, they high-fived and tossed their beers and collected their bets.

It was indeed a glorious day. Blessed indeed was deAngelo Freeman.

Victory in Christ and on the field achieved, deAngelo fell to his knees as was his custom, striking the reverent pose that was his signature move.

As the people celebrated, he, too, celebrated, tucking the football under his arm and bowing his head to give thanks to the Lord.

As he prayed, the high priests of the sports world, sitting in the press booths atop the stadium, in turn praised deAngelo, claiming with jubilation in their voices that his talents were indeed extraordinary and giving thanks that America was so blessed to have a man like deAngelo Freeman, a moral compass for other young men, a humble man, a man of family, a man of faith, a man of God.

The stadium buzzed, vibrating like bees in a hive, each on high alert, each screaming to be heard above all the others.

But deAngelo remained still - still crouching, still praying, still giving thanks - when tight end Bruce Peltski fell on his back to bear hug him out of his trance.

But deAngelo did not move.

As Peltski stepped back, the Jumbotrons began a slow zoom towards the man in prayer, tighter and tighter, with amazing clarity, lighted and illuminated so that the image of deAngelo shone in extraordinary detail, zooming in until tens of millions of spectators in this great country of ours could see the individual drops of sweat on the back of deAngelo's neck, dead center, in the middle of the screen.

The zoom stopped in extreme close up and the image froze.

One by one, they became quiet. And one by one they started pointing, until everyone pointed to the same spot, to the drops of bright, red, sparkling blood creeping down the chin strap of deAngelo Freeman.

Medics rushed in.

Dr. Milton Lieberman, the team physician, released the strap and pulled away the helmet.

The video feed was cut.

The monitors in the stadium flashed off.

And all across America screens went black, replaced seconds later by a commercial for Bud Lite.

- - -

The next day, Monday, Goldwater and Cruze filed suit in California to initiate a Class Action against Susan Nicole "Suzze" Osmond [née Gilmore], the estate of Joel Richard Osmond, and Camels in a Haystack Incorporated aka "Prosperity Cathedral" in the amount of $150 million, alleging fraud, deception and misappropriation of funds, on behalf of yet-to-be-named defendants.

- - -

Later that week, nursery schools and day care centers around the country received boxes of stuffed dolls in the image of Baby Jesus from Saddle River World Outreach. A tag assured that the fabric was hypoallergenic, that the materials were safe and that the dolls were proudly Made in the U.S.A. When squeezed, the doll said, 'Jesus loves you,' 'Honor thy father and thy mother,' and a half-dozen other family and child related verses. It was estimated that, in total, over half a million dolls were distributed within a 48 hour period. The children loved them.

| In the Beginning

"WHAT DO PEOPLE WANT, SON?"

What do people want, Son? That was always the topic, always the lesson. Give people what they want. Not what they need. What they want. The two are rarely the same.

What do people want, Son? Joel Osmond had learned the lesson well.

1995 was a good year for America. The DOW exploded. The NASDAQ screamed past 1000 on its way to successive all-time highs. Everybody had a job. Home prices soared. Drugs were plentiful. Netscape Navigator gave birth to Internet Explorer and so Internet porn was born. Bill Clinton was busy poking bimbos with Cuban cigars. And a pretty young Oxford graduate named Blythe Masters invented the Credit Default Swap, but it would be ten more years before her spawn was let loose to destroy life as we know it.

1995 was Joel Osmond's graduation year.

"What do people want, Son?"

"To go to heaven and live forever in the Kingdom of God, Father."

"No, Son. That is their reward for dying. While they live on this earth people want one thing."

"What is that, Father?"

"Prosperity." Father said it again, with reverence, almost at a whisper. "*Pros-per-ity.*"

"Money, Father?"

"No, not money, Son. Money is vulgar. And not riches, Son. Riches are a sin."

"Then what is Prosperity, Father?"

"Prosperity is more, Son. More than the man next to you. All it takes to make any man happy is to have more than the man next to him. That's *Prosperity*."

Father delivered unto them what they wanted. Sometimes it was real estate. Sometimes it was insurance. Sometimes it was whatever else was at hand. But whatever it was, it was always endorsed by God. Why would you buy anything less?

Father was a lay minister, a man of the people. He knew what people wanted. People didn't want the truth. And anyway, what is the truth? He knew that the only real truth is to be found in scripture, not in logic. Father studied the scientific sales techniques of Zig Zeigler, the Prophet of Prosperity for super salesmen everywhere. He knew that people didn't want facts. Facts can be twisted and turned to prove anything, so facts prove nothing. He knew that people, all people, rich people and poor people alike want one thing more than anything else. More.

Keep your teeth brushed, your shoes shined and your hair combed, Father taught Son. Your toenails don't matter. Nobody sees your toes. What's inside doesn't matter. They can't see inside you and you can't do anything about what's inside anyway. But on the outside, look so clean you squeak. Because dirty people see clean and what do they think Son? *Pros-per-ity*.

And, although God's grace fell bountifully onto Father for all his good deeds, Father and Son often moved from town to town, county to county, in the middle of the night so as not to have to account for themselves or the blessings they bestowed. The process servers from real estate deals gone bad or investment opportunities turned sour were an evil force that kept them on the move, for God's work is never accounted for.

And so it came to pass that a few days after Joel Osmond's sixteenth birthday, Father left the room he and Joel currently shared at the Motel 6 just outside of Uvalde, Texas to join his Lord Jesus in Heaven, the ticket purchased with a massive coronary.

As soon as the body bag was zipped shut and rolled out the door, Joel rifled through Father's suitcase, tossed his sandwich bag full of neatly rolled marijuana cigarettes along with a half pack of Camels, three Magnum condoms and a copy of Penthouse magazine into his own duffle bag, stuck the keys in his pocket and headed out the door.

Joel had just inherited Father's Lincoln Continental convertible with two-hundred and twenty-seven thousand miles. He tossed his bag in the back, adjusted the six-way power seat, dropped the top, rolled down the windows and headed out of town. He punched in the cigarette lighter and slipped a cassette into the player. As the lighter popped out, the music came on. Father's favorite. Carlos Santana. *Black Magic Woman*. He turned it up, lit a joint, took a deep slow drag, hacked, coughed, ran onto the shoulder and snatched the car back onto the road again.

He took another hit, put the joint in the ashtray, turned up the music even more, balanced the speakers, maxed the bass, and leaned back with his right arm stretched across the top of the long bench seat with his left hand draped nonchalantly across the steering wheel. He reached down, took another hit, cranked the music up as loud as it would go and drove into another world.

And it was on this very day, at this magical moment that Joel Osmond fell in love for the first time.

With himself.

| Lonely Boy

AND SO, UTILIZING THE LESSONS HE LEARNED from Father, the Master, Son became, not the most successful real estate broker in West Texas, or hottest investment advisor in the greater Dallas metro area, but the most celebrated young evangelist in the country, often compared to a short but youthful Billy Graham.

In his quest to capture souls for God, like Father before him, he moved around, from church to church, town to town, elevating his stature and his bank account at every stop.

He sold what he was.

He was what he sold.

One begat the other.

Joel Osmond was God's messenger on Earth, the message was Prosperity, and there was nowhere to go but up.

Only one thing was missing he often thought to himself as he pulled up the covers and turned off the lights, most nights in a different bed, always alone.

Someone with whom he could share in the glory.

Someone with whom he could share his unquenchable desire to celebrate his prosperous life with those in want.

Someone just like him.

Someone with good teeth, great hair and a big smile.

Someone with perfect breasts and a nice, firm behind.

Just thinking about it, about her, whoever she was, lying

there beside him filled him with a desire that was hard to satisfy.

Only Father's music came close.

So Joel would plug in the headphones of his portable cassette player and listen to his man Carlos as he played his instrument long into the night.

| Playmates

JOEL OSMOND WAS ON HIS WAY to becoming a star.

In reality, he was on his way to the assembly hall at Bob Jones University where he was billed as a *rising* star, but to Joel that was just a detail. Four years on the road had finally brought him here, ready to make his big move, ready to make his grand appearance, ready for the big leagues.

Only one thing stood in his way as he walked by himself across the campus green to join others of his generation where they would each promote themselves as evangelists of a new age of Christian belief.

And that one thing was a great piece of ass.

And as it turned out, it was standing right in the middle of the walkway twenty feet in front of him, looking the other way, swaying to an inaudible beat.

It looked like it had no intention of moving out of the way, so Joel walked right up behind it and snatched the plugs from its ears.

The girl swung around to meet him, standing a full head taller than he.

"Girl, you know how much trouble I can get you into for this?"

He shook the headset in front of her face and then stuck the plugs into his own ears. He listened silently, bobbing his head to the beat while she – whoever she was – acted surprised and disgruntled.

He pulled one of the plugs from his ear and spoke half to himself, half to the poor girl with the dazed look, "Old fashioned and nasty. Breaking all the rules. Lord, that's just the way I like it."

What he meant by that was:

OLD FASHIONED – in that she was listening to a guy around since the '60s, Carlos Santana, a man old enough to be her daddy and by pure coincidence, Joel's favorite guitar player of all time. Joel tried to explain his fascination with Carlos to her but she either was not interested or simply didn't get it. Either way, she said nothing while Joel looked her up and down, thought she might not be his intellectual equal but decided to give her a chance anyway.

NASTY – because she was listening to *Black Magic Woman* from Carlos Santana's *Abraxas* album.

"Girl, do you have any idea what this is all about?"

"Why no, Mr. Osmond, I haven't a clue, pray tell why don't you enlighten me?"

Joel listened through the one plug still in his ear and played air guitar as he enunciated the passage he had memorized from Father's copy of the Gnostic texts: *We questioned it, berated it, made love to it, prayed to it. We called it mother, called it whore and slut, called it our beloved, called it Abraxas.*

Whoever wrote that, Joel told the girl, sure knew what women were all about.

BREAKING ALL THE RULES – because listening to an illegal CD

player was enough to get that gorgeous butt kicked right out of BJU. But not to worry, young lady. He was in control of the situation and not prone to getting pretty young girls in trouble, at least not for a first offense.

Joel closed his eyes, played his imaginary guitar and sang along just loud enough that she, and nobody else, could hear, *you got your spell on me...you a black magic woman and you trying to make a devil out of me.*

Yes, Lord, Joel sure did like this woman he'd just happened to run into on the way to becoming a star. And what an amazing coincidence that they both liked the same music. Only one answer could there be, heaven sent. He was getting a boner just thinking about it.

He put down his imaginary guitar, took his bow before his imaginary audience and thrust out his hand, "Hi, my name's Joel. Joel Osmond."

She took his hand in a firm, professional grip and said, "Susan Gilmore, Mr. Osmond. Your reputation precedes you. It is such a pleasure to meet you. I have been hoping for such a long time to meet you. It really is a pleasure, to meet you, I mean."

It occurred to her that she might be taking this submissive bullshit a little too far.

Joel looked straight ahead at her breasts in response.

As great as her ass was, her breasts were not.

It wasn't that Joel was a hard-core tittie man, but that he understood the monetary value of perceived perfection. He liked big titties, big hair, big teeth, a big smile and a big personality. He thought they fit in just fine with his big plans.

Susan Gilmore eased her less than perfect breasts a few

inches forward until they were staring him in the face and asked Joel Osmond if he was maybe her light on the road to the promised land. It went right over his head.

Keep it simple, she reminded herself.

"Are you probing me *Mizz* – Joel strung out the word for effect – Gilmore?"

Bait offered.

Bait accepted.

At that point, she knew she would be coasting all the way.

Six months later Ms. Susan Gilmore became Mrs. Susan Osmond, still a virgin, sort of, never having been penetrated, exactly, never vaginally, completely – at least not by Joel.

Six months later still, with a good set of D-cups, some serious tooth whitening, a thousand-dollar hairdo, her own personal logo and color scheme, and a name that could be trademarked – and The New and Improved Susan Osmond was introduced to the world as the perfect preacher's perfect wife. Suzze was born, created by her maker in his own image.

After six months more of praying together, singing together, dancing together, hitting their marks together and screwing a lot, Joel and Suzze bound their script and took their show on the road. *The Road to Prosperity*, Joel named it, making sure to copyright every page.

They never slowed down.

They never looked back.

Those starving African babies she had so wanted to devote her life to, helping them to find nourishment in the Lord, would just have to wait.

| Prosperity

Soo-zee, Soo-zee, Soo-zee.

The chanting began even before the congregation could see the object of their affection.

Look this way, Suzze. Suzze, Suzze over here.

Joel and Suzze Osmond strolled into the 17,000 seat Prosperity Cathedral like they owned the place. Mostly, they did. *The Road to Prosperity* had been straight and fast. In little more than a decade they had built their organization from the ground up with donations from hundreds of thousands of people who believed that, by blessing Joel – who they knew had a special relationship with their Lord and Savior, Jesus Christ – they would, in turn, be blessed. Money flowed in by the buckets full and Joel and Suzze invested it in the surest bet they could find – themselves.

Truth be told, there were more than a few sizable contributions from boards of directors who might someday need a trusted spokesperson to help with legislative issues, or environmental regulations, or union busting. They knew, these captains of industry, that it never hurts to have God on your side and that, with his message of free-wheeling consumerism, Joel could deliver.

And blessed his followers were.

With their easy credit and second mortgages, they bought more and more with the blessings Joel bestowed.

As the plumbers and roofers and mortgage brokers with the skills and trades and connections that responded to and benefited from the real estate bubble, they prospered as never before.

And that Prosperity was not just a blessing for their hard work but a reward from God who smiled upon them and their cathedral with more generosity than was bestowed upon any church since the Popes of Rome ruled the western world.

In a dozen mirror cathedrals across America, another in England, two in Africa, and more pending in Central and South America, where Joel personified the American dream, hundreds of thousands gathered to praise Joel, surrounded by larger than life video screens with digital sound so crisp and clear that when Joel spoke his voice was as if he were standing beside you, and speaking only to you, and blessing you above all others in this, his most blessed of flocks.

The Lord blessed Joel and made him more prosperous than Father could have ever imagined – for Son learned one very important lesson that Father himself never understood. It was a lesson he learned from the pages of Fortune Magazine and the Wall Street Journal, a lesson that all the richest men in the world knew: If you want to make even *more* money, cut out the middleman. There's no need to sell insurance in order to have a vessel from which to bestow blessings upon those in want, no need to sell bogus lots where they can spend their golden years basking in the glory of God.

Just sell them God.

Just sell them what they want, *Prosperity*.

Indeed, Joel transcended Father, taking his message to a higher level. Gone was the old school - person to person, door to door. In was the new school - *branding*.

By studying the best minds of Madison Avenue – McDonald's and Coca-Cola, Starbucks and the Jolly Green Giant – Joel learned that every great brand must appeal, not on a rational level, but on an emotional level as well. Emotion is the key. Not everybody has a brain. Not everybody can think. Most people can't. But everybody has feelings. Joel learned that the product itself can be third rate in every respect as long as people identify with it and feel positive toward it.

He had the algorithm and it was perfect. On the Road to Prosperity, he was their path to salvation, she was their ticket to paradise. But that too was too cerebral, too abstract. He had to come down market.

Joel knew what matters most is how your brand is *perceived*, and – *if you are the brand and the brand is you* – as it is with the giants, Martha Stewart, and Oprah Winfrey and her birthlings, Dr. Phil and Dr. Oz – then you must craft your persona to appeal on a subliminal level. You must dig deep into the reptilian brain, down where the survival instinct alone rules. You must be more than simply who you are. You must be more, even, than who they want you to be. You must be who they themselves want to be. You must be the ideal they strive for.

Then it occurred to him as if by a blinding light. No need to reinvent the wheel. No need to craft anew what waits to be copied. Build your success upon the shoulders of giants.

At his Eternal Game of Wheel of Fortune, he would channel Pat Sajak and she would follow in the footsteps of Vanna White.

Every Sunday, Joel shared a different version of the same story, how his own personal path of hard work and sacrifice, of optimism and perseverance, made him the man he is today.

He implored his flock to join him and Suzze in enjoying the unimaginable blessings that only the Lord can provide, the happiness that only financial security – the cornerstone of Prosperity – can grant.

"Be humble. Bow before the Lord. Join Him and His personal blessings for a life without want, here, now, on this Earth. Heaven is for the next life. Heaven is the *final* blessing, don't pass up the bounty he holds for you on this Earth. God wants you to enjoy his blessings. *Here! Now! Today!*"

Every Sunday, and in each of his books which collectively sold over 100 million copies worldwide, Joel Osmond told of growing up with a father who struggled. A simple country preacher, Father traveled the backroads of West Texas looking for converts, for lost souls he might bring to God. How he worked and struggled to gain the trust and respect of everyone he encountered and how he helped them find the faith that was always inside them without any expectation of reward. Father taught him not to seek Prosperity but to trust in the Lord and let the Lord grant Prosperity unto you.

And when Father died, Joel knew that the Lord would find a special place in Heaven for this simple country preacher who was also his beloved dad.

Joel told his story over and over again, how he, Son, followed in Father's footsteps, how life was hard and the rewards were few. How, one night, when looking up at the multitude of stars in the heavens, he wondered aloud, Lord, where is my reward? Lord, where is my Prosperity here on this Earth?

And then he would tell the story of his first car. It was a used car but looked like new, smelled like new. A Lincoln

Continental which belonged to a less than honest real estate salesman who went bust because his heart was not pure.

And he told them how he asked unto the Lord, "If I buy this car, Lord, will you make the payments?"

And the congregation would laugh a muted little laugh.

Joel knew well not to let a few facts get in the way of his communion with the Lord's people.

And he would continue with the story and the congregation would laugh another muted little laugh until Suzze stepped forward and waved her arms and opened her hands to God, laughing and smiling, smiling and laughing out loud until the laughter grew contagious and they all waved their arms in unison and laughed louder still.

And if they did not laugh loudly enough or respond exuberantly enough, Suzze would cup her hands over her ears, I...can't...hear...you, always the cheerleader, always the beautiful bride.

And Joel would say, "Laugh! But always remember, the Lord is on your side. He wants you to have all that you need to do his work on this Earth. "Hey, sometimes you need a new car!

"So stop now, and ask yourself, What do you need? What do you need to help others find glory in God?

"Now ask for it.

"Ask God.

"Right here!

"Right now!

"Ask God to help you so that you can help God.

"Ask!

"Out loud!

"Let the Lord hear your prayers! Ask for the Lord's blessings! Just ask!"

And on Suzze's cue, the congregation would raise their arms higher still and close their eyes and whisper their prayers like a thousand buzzing bees, each in search of their own personal nectar. And the buzzing would turn into a mumble and the mumbles into voices, and the voices into chanting and the chanting into singing and it rolled throughout the cathedral in waves, louder and louder.

And Joel would cry out, his microphone now at full volume, *"He's listening. You know he's listening. He's listening to you, right now."*

And the voices whispered and shouted and laughed and cried along with Joel in their joy for the blessings they knew awaited them, if not here, now, today, then soon, for soon the Lord would see they were ready, soon the Lord would see that they were worthy of the Prosperity he was so eager to bestow.

And when Joel had them on high, he would bring them low again.

He stood.

And waited.

Head bowed.

Motionless. Waiting for the audience to quiet itself until all that could be heard were muted sobs punctuated by random coughs.

Quiet.

Somber.

Reflective.

Then he would pick it up again, the climax just a minute away.

He beamed.

He looked to Suzze and his look alone was evidence of his undying love and affection. He held her gaze until the audience burst into applause, a celebration of the life that they and they shared with Joel and Suzze Osmond.

Confident again, he gazed upward to the far corners, to the farthest rows, his smile radiant, the speakers now tuned a pitch lower, his voice deep and slow, very slow, and sincere, word by careful word, a father telling his daughter a bedtime story.

"Only you stand in the way of the Lord's blessings.

"Only you stand in the way of Prosperity.

"Only you.

"The Lord awaits you.

"The Lord is steadfast.

"It's all up to you.

"Quietly now.

"Gently now.

"Tell the Lord your time has come."

- - -

And the Lord God had indeed made Joel Prosperous.

And with that Prosperity had come Suzze, his young and beautiful and exuberant wife, so full of spirit, so kind of heart, so natural of body, a companion, a mate, a partner in the Lord, an extraordinary woman who walked alongside her beloved husband, knowing that all the blessings he received, the Lord wanted her to receive as well.

"It is yours, it is all yours if only you believe."

"If only you *believe*," he wept, naturally, sincerely, tears streaming down his cheeks.

"If only you *believe*," he whispered, eyes closed channeling the Lord.

"If only you *believe*."

"If only you *believe*." His voice quavered.

"If only you *believe*." His arms dropped.

"If only…" His shoulders slumped.

Suzze noticed a pulse, a drop of blood bobbing up and down inside Joel's ear, until, with the next beat of his heart it overflowed in a trickle that dripped off his earlobe and onto his shoulder, too small on his dark suit for anyone else to see.

"If only you believe, my brothers and sisters." His lips moved but there was no sound.

He turned to Suzze.

"If only…"

| Pop Secret

THE SMARTEST MAN IN THE WORLD walked into the Oval Office where the President of the United States waited to greet him. Even though he was the President's personally appointed National Science Advisor, the president had never actually met him. Didn't need to. Science just got in the way of doing business. And anyway, the president wasn't sure he cared for his type. Professor Laurence Gelb, Nobel Prize winner, a scientist's scientist, was also known to have a weak spot for poetry and classical music so the consensus in the administration was that he had to be the Q-word.

The president picked up a copy of Time magazine. Gelb's photo and the caption 'Is This the Smartest Man in the World?' were on the cover. He held it at arm's length, comparing the photo with what stood in front of him.

"What's that guy's name?"

"Who, Mr. President?"

"The Michelin guy? The tire man? You know who I'm talking about?"

Gelb hesitated, asking himself if he should suffer the indignity of an answer, even if it was the President of the United States asking the question.

"Bibendum, sir. His name's Bibendum."

Indeed, Larry Gelb knew exactly where the president was going. He'd heard it a thousand times. The Michelin tire man.

The Pillsbury doughboy. Casper the friendly ghost. Just look in the mirror. White as a sheet. Beady little black eyes. Hairless, with rolls of flesh, not fat, but rolls of pithy flesh, one roll rolling onto the other all improbably contained in a bespoke suit. That was Larry Gelb.

He had heard that the president was a complete asshole and now he knew it firsthand.

What he wanted to tell the president was that he even knew the Latin derivation of the name, *Nunc est bibendum* which means *Now is the time to drink,* and that it was from Horace, Book 1, Ode 27, as a matter of fact. After all, he was the smartest man in the world, why not act the part? But why bother? With Augustus Jefferson, it would be as if casting pearls before swine. How could a black man, even if he was the President, especially if he was the President, be such a redneck?

"So who's your favorite?" asked the president.

"Favorite what, Mr. President? Favorite advertising character? Favorite tire man? Favorite trademark? Favorite what?"

"Tel-e-evangelist. The president made a point of enunciating between the syllables. Which one's your favorite? Of all time?"

Although he had no idea at all where this one was going, Gelb thought for a minute, "Well, I'll have to go with Swaggart."

"Jimmy? Why Jimmy? Why not Creflo Dollar? And his sweet wife Taffi? Friends of mine, I might add. Or how about Eddie Long or Pastor Steve? Or Billy's boy Franklin? Nah, I take that back, Franklin's a lightweight, not in the same league with Creflo, buried his own dead mama beside a talking cow in an amusement park for Christ's sake. Guess he never heard that Honor thy Mother part."

"The cow's still mooin' and the money's still flowin', Praise Jesus." Gelb couldn't resist.

"Don't tell me Brother Franklin really said that," asked the president.

"No, Mr. President. He didn't. I did," said Gelb.

"So, why Jimmy? Why Jimmy Swaggart?"

Gelb wanted to make a point of sounding objective, "I guess it's his resilience, Mr. President. Here's a man caught red handed sticking a vibrator up a whore's pucker in a cheap motel…"

The president cut in, "He was anointing her with Vaseline. That's how they found him out. She was in there jacked up doggie style hollering Oh Jesus, Oh Jesus, Oh Jesus, and they peeked through the window to see what the commotion was all about, saw Jimmy with his sweatpants around his ankles with his little pecker pointed to heaven warming her up to receive the Lord. At least that's what I heard. Don't know if you can believe it or not."

The president finished talking to himself. Gelb picked up where he left off, "…and he's still going strong, like that drum-banging bunny rabbit."

"Hey, the man wept. Live. On TV. Real tears." The president craned his neck up and put his knuckles on his cheeks, flicking his fingers up and down like falling tears and cried, "Boohoo, boohoo, I have sinned, boohoo-hoo-hoo."

Chaim Herschfeld, the president's former campaign manager, now Chief of Staff, entered unannounced reading and talking as he walked through the door.

"Here's what we know so far Mr. President, which isn't much."

Herschfeld then outlined the last days of God's favorite couple. Joel Osmond wasn't hurting, not that anybody could tell. Bad economy, but that just made things better for him. As usual, his wife, forever the bimbo, was fighting off another lawsuit by a little person she insulted or bullied or pushed around. But none of that explained what happened. As best they could tell, there were no hostiles in the audience. No one had threatened Osmond's life. No one out of the ordinary, anyway. He hadn't picked a fight with the terrorists, wasn't a stone cold fuck up like Franklin Graham. Joel Osmond was in it for the money, everybody knew that. His crowd wanted a piece of what he had, not a piece of him.

"So did he really blow up?" asked the president. "His head really explode? Anybody hear a pop or a bang? What did they see? They must have it all on video."

"Yeah, we got it on video," said Herschfeld. "Osmond gets a nose bleed…"

"Ear bleed," corrected Gelb. "And no, his head didn't explode. His eyes popped out and much of his pre-frontal cortex shot out of his nose but his head didn't explode."

"Ear bleed, nose bleed, what's the difference?" asked Herschfeld.

"Just trying to be precise," said Gelb. "Details matter. His head didn't explode. His skull cracked, like a hardboiled egg."

The president read from the report on his desk, "Says here a guy named Pete who was standing in the third row said it looked just like a muskmelon that got shot with a .357 magnum. 'Ka-boom and it was gone' is what he said. What's wrong with that? Ever shot one of them bad boys? Ka-boom. That's plausible."

The president continued, "FOX says it's the terrorists, first shot fired in the War on Christianity."

"Wasn't shot, Mr. President, no matter what some bubba on FOX says," said Herschfeld. "We know that for sure."

"CNN's gone all conspiracy theory," said the president. "Saw it on TV last night. Had that guy on writes all them conspiracy books. What's his name, Herschbo?"

"Brown," said Herschfeld. "Dan Brown. The Da Vinci Code."

"That's right," said the president, "Said Jesus had a red-headed mama. Leonardo Da Vinci was his brother. What kind of crap is that? I saw the movie. Jesus had a red-headed mama, so what?"

"Red-headed *wife*, Mr. President." Larry Gelb corrected him. "Jesus had a red-headed wife. Some sort of Scottish princess."

"Wife?"

"Wife, not mother."

"I missed that. Red-headed wife, red-headed mama, still don't amount to nothing. And I still don't know how Leonardo Da Vinci was related to Jesus Christ."

"I don't think Dan Brown killed him, Mr. President," said Herschfeld, putting the issue to rest.

"Okay, so this room full of bible huggers is praying for a new flatscreen or a bass boat when Smileyboy's head does a cherry bomb and nobody hears nothing and we've got no idea what's going on. Jeez boys, I can't run with that, can I?"

"We're modeling algorithms now," Gelb reassured him.

"What's your best guess?" asked the president.

"Autopsy is inconclusive," said Gelb. "They're missing a lot of tissue. Not much to work with."

"All I want is an answer," said the president. "It doesn't have to be a good answer, it doesn't have to be the right answer, just an answer our base will believe. Can't stand for them to start blaming it on us. Primaries next year. We're still the party of God, want to keep it that way."

The president looked toward the door. "That's all gentlemen."

Gelb and Herschfeld turned in unison to leave.

Halfway out the door the president called after them, "Oh yeah, Osmond's wife, Suzette. What happened to her?"

"Suzze, Sir. S-U-Z-Z-E. Sounds like Susie," said Herschfeld.

"So where is Ms. S-U-Z-Z-E, sounds like Susie? Don't they figure she knows something? Be good to talk to her, don't you think?"

"Vanished Mr. President. Thin air. A mystery unto itself," said Herschfeld. "We got the boys looking for her but nothing yet. Won't be long."

"Have you tried heaven?" asked Gelb.

"What?" The president didn't understand the question.

Herschfeld grabbed Gelb by the arm, "A joke, Mr. President. Larry made a funny."

"Did you know her, Mr. President? Suzze?" asked Gelb.

"Nah, never met her. But I saw her on the shopping channel a couple of times selling holy wrinkle cream. Never thought she was too bright. But she sure did have great tits."

| Not My Head

THE ON-SITE INVESTIGATION into the incident at Prosperity Cathedral was over, for the time being at least.

The press, the police, the National Security people were all gone except for an armed guard by each door and Dub Whittaker who, unknown to most and ignored by all, still patrolled the parking lot in his prized Prosperity Cathedral Security windbreaker, a gift to him from Mr. and Mrs. Joel Osmond on the occasion of his seventy-fifth birthday celebration, which, regrettably, they could not attend, but their hearts were with him nonetheless.

It was freezing, too cold for the windbreaker, but Dub was a prideful man. Yes, he could sit in the car with the heater on, but that wasn't what they paid him for, even though they didn't actually pay him, never had. No mind, when he accepted the job, he accepted the responsibilities that went with it.

He was making his rounds as he had for years. Nobody told him to stop.

Dub reconnoitered the back lot where the tour buses and limousines were parked. Strands of yellow Do Not Cross police tape that had broken loose and caught on the shrubs flapped in the wind like streamers after a parade.

There it was.

A brand new Integra Anthem Eagle Coach, a Mark IV Patriot.

Dub was there when they delivered it, he told his friends at Seniors Bingo. He looked it up on the Internet. Forty-three feet long. Three wide-screen TVs. Over $400,000 new and still they had it customized. Three-hundred thousand dollars for the interior. Two-hundred thousand for electronics and security. Another hundred thousand a year for drivers. Close to a million bucks by the time they got it on the road, he bragged to the old timers, parked right there in his parking lot. But Joel and Miss Suzze, well, with all their hard work, they deserved it, Miss Suzze especially, with her condition and all.

He strolled over to the giant cream-colored bus festooned with pink and blue and lavender streamers flowing between the letters on the side. *Prosperity Has Arrived*, it read. Though they were painted on, the streamers looked like they were fluttering down the side of the bus and blowing in the wind even when the bus was standing still. *Now that's a paint job.*

Dub looked up at the gold-tinted windows, too high for him to peek through. He walked around to the far side of the motor home. The ramp was extended and the door was open an inch.

When is a door not a door? When it is ajar.

Dub sensed a security issue and decided to investigate.

He looked both ways to make sure no one was watching and then stepped quickly into the bus.

He felt it. The hum of the pumps and generators was inaudible, the frequency so low that it was felt, not heard, like alveolar air, the sound between breaths. It surrounded him, the calm, the sense that this place existed in a world apart from any he could imagine, a place where nothing could go wrong.

He kept his hands in his pockets as he peered into the cockpit.

He stepped down into the sunken living room.

It was warm inside. Fragrant.

He heard a chirp, like a bird. And then another, like a different kind of bird.

Dub always dreamed of a simple retirement on the road, a small trailer to pull behind his van, he and the wife free as birds, each evening spent overlooking a magnificent sunset somewhere in this big, beautiful country of ours.

The birds chirped again, more of them, faintly, like a rainforest far away. It was like birds if the birds were in Heaven.

He took his hands out of his pockets.

Ms. Suzze had gone missing, abducted by terrorists or held captive by a rival congregation or who knows what. But he, Dub Whittaker knew that she was in here, somewhere. He could sense it. Should he sit and wait, silent and motionless until she made a sound?

Common sense would say, simply call out her name and she would answer, eager to be rescued.

Uncommon sense, the kind that Dub knew he possessed from reading every Dean Koontz novel ever published, told him that a plot twist was in order, that things were not what they seemed, that something spooky was at play.

He had experienced it firsthand. He was the man who ran into the church when everybody else was running out, screaming and flailing, running out of every door and across the parking lot, nobody looking back, afraid to look back lest they turn to salt, some rushing to their cars, others running, just running, running away.

No sir, the old rules did not apply. Not here. Not today. Maybe not ever again.

Miss Suzze did not want to be found. Dub knew that. But she had to be, for her own good, and it was he, Dub Whitaker who had the secret knowledge to delve deep beneath the obvious and find the solution that others could not see.

After a long life, mundane by any standards, his destiny was upon him. Fate thrust him here, at this time, in this place, to rescue the object of his obsession, thereby melding their souls, a bond that henceforth they and only they would share.

He walked to the door of the galley. Others might call it a kitchen but on a moving vehicle Dub knew it was called a galley.

He opened the door to the oven.

Then the door to the refrigerator.

He looked through the cabinets.

Not there.

He inched his way through the vehicle, stopped, then peeked into the control room – no enclosed spaces, nowhere to hide.

He continued on, step by careful step through the rosewood door marked 'Private' and into the couple's personal quarters.

He stepped into the master bath.

He noticed the TP with Suzze's logo on it and how the end was folded to a point. Unused, he surmised.

He ran his hand across the seat of her commode. He may have sensed a vibration. He wasn't sure.

He fingered her name, embroidered on her hand towels.

He smelled her perfume and put a dab behind his ears.

He entered her dressing room, silently on the plush carpet, one slow step at a time as dozens of mini-spots activated by motion sensors sparkled to life. Behind tinted glass doors, duplicate dresses arranged by color; pink, blue, and lavender, hung in perfect order.

Her shoes were here.

Her bras were here.

No panties.

No panties? He reached for a drawer to open it but his touch alone caused it to slide out with a low hum, illuminated inside by soft lights. Empty. No panties. Where would she keep her panties?

What could it mean? It was what was *missing* that had meaning. What was *found* did not. CSI had taught him that.

Then, he found a single pair – on the floor behind the commode. A single pair of panties. Soiled. On the floor. No other panties to be found. He held the underwear in his palm and rolled it between his fingers expecting the tactile stimulation to provide a clue, perhaps to activate his clairvoyant senses.

He resisted the urge to bring them to his face for fear that someone would see him even though he knew no one else was there. Being seen sniffing a woman's underwear, any woman's underwear but especially Miss Suzze's would be a humiliation he could never endure. Instead, he held them close to his breast letting the aroma waft upward.

He rested them back on the floor, making a point of placing them just as he found them.

A few more silent steps and he was in the bedroom.

On the bed lay a nightgown, laid out for the evening, arranged as if it were styled for a fashion shoot. A phantom had slept here. Now only her most intimate possessions remained. Had she been here and gone? No, the box of mints on her pillow was unopened. Dub's powers of reasoning were growing exponentially.

By stark contrast, the closet to the bedroom was completely empty except for a vintage, lime green Samsonite overnight case, the sort, he knew, that teenage girls used to carry for overnight stays and pajama parties.

There were automatic drawers under the platform bed. He waved his hand and they opened. Inside, he saw only strange things, rubber things, things he knew existed but things he had never actually seen, certainly never touched. No need to delve deeper. No clues here. He waved the drawer shut and immediately forgot what he had seen.

Suzze Osmond was nowhere to be found.

Resigned to his failure, he lay on the bed, on his side, knees bent, head on his elbow gazing onto the nightgown which he encapsulated with his body, protecting it from harm. He spoke to her and she spoke to him.

They both agreed that he had done his duty and that now it was best to go before someone came in and found them, discovered them, here in bed together. Miss Suzze's reputation was at stake and as much as they cared for each other, and for so long had waited for this moment, they must keep their secrets. Go now, yes, time to go.

Dub Whittaker rose and walked down the central hall as slowly as he could so as to prolong his leaving.

As he opened the door and stuck his head outside to look left, then right, then left again to be certain he was not being observed, something gave him pause. Why was a lime green Samsonite overnight case sitting alone in the middle of the floor in an empty closet?

He traced his steps back the way he had come, this time with purpose and determination. He sat on the bed without acknowledging the negligee's presence, reached into the closet, retrieved the overnight case, sat it in his lap, fiddled with the snaps and opened the lid. A band of hundred dollar bills fell on the floor.

How much money? He didn't know. But a lot, a whole lot, thousands at least, definitely hundreds of thousands, could be millions, enough money to fill his pockets and line the waistband of his sans-a-belt trousers.

When his pants were full he zipped his jacket to the chin and dumped it in, the lumps of cash making the jacket bulge around his waist and under his arms.

He paused, reached into the bulge, took out three or four packs of bills and put them back into the overnight case so it wouldn't look like there had been a robbery, a trick he learned from an old Perry Mason episode.

He returned the overnight case exactly as he found it and gingerly walked back the length of the vehicle and out the door, every movement from beginning to end captured on button cameras mounted throughout the unit which automatically recorded his most tender moments every step of the way.

He stepped out of the bus, closed the door, then opened it again leaving it cracked an inch or two, just as he found it.

This time, he was more cautious. He not only looked left and right, he dropped to his knees and looked under the bus, looking for feet on the other side, private eye style. He knew the tricks of the trade. No feet, no people. He was safe.

What he saw instead was one of the lavender streamers billowing out the back of the bus.

But how could that be?

The pink and blue and lavender streamers were painted on. They couldn't come loose. He stood and ran his fingers over the side of the bus checking the paint job to make sure.

He walked to the back of the bus and crouched on his hands and knees again, hard to do with the lumps of money squeezing into his belly.

It seemed like the slip of lavender was attached to something.

He tugged at it to see what is was but it didn't give.

He pulled a little harder and when it still didn't budge he stuck his head underneath to see what it was attached to.

It was dark under the bus. He couldn't make it out.

He got down on his belly – too old to be doing this, he said to himself – so that his head was well under the bus so that his eyes could adjust to the shadows.

When his eyes came back into focus, he noticed that the lavender silk chiffon was attached to Suzze Osmond who was frozen in a fetal position, wedged up into an impossibly small space within the bowels of the mechanics of the drivetrain. How in the world could she have got run over and sucked up in there?

"Miss Suzze, Miss Suzze, how did you get yourself up under here girl? What you doin' here Miss Suzze?"

He inched his way a little closer, crawling on his belly. As he slid closer, eyes now adjusted, he could see her pale, white skin and the frost on her eyelids and knew for sure that his beloved Suzze was frozen dead as a doornail.

He scooted in reverse from under the bus and fast as a seventy-five-year-old man can run with thirty pounds of hundred dollar bills bouncing around his waist, ran to the guard by the front doors, waving his arms and yelling to call the police, call an ambulance, get some help, help now, hurry, and without waiting for a response ran back to the bus.

Just as quickly he scooted back under, thinking that, no matter what, this poor woman, even in death, should not be left alone.

After a few slow, intentional blinks to get his eyes once again adjusted to the darkness, he noticed that Suzze Osmond's body had dropped to the pavement. Her arms and legs were tucked tightly underneath her. Her face was flat against the asphalt. Before he could control what he was thinking – for he would never have allowed himself to consciously think anything unflattering about Miss Suzze – it crossed his mind that she looked just like a fallen, lavender bat, road kill frozen to the pavement on a frosty night.

He lay there, under the bus, watching her, motionless, waiting for the sound of the sirens that would relieve him of his duty when he noticed a long, thin strand of spittle, delicate as a spider's web, drip from the corner of her mouth. After seeing another drop of crystal clear saliva, he scooted closer and was sure he could feel the heat from her body even through the bone-numbing chill under the bus.

Dub Whittaker called to her again, softly now, without tension or urgency, "Miss Suzze, just give me your hand now. Hold on to me, Miss Suzze. Can you hear me, Miss Suzze? Just take my hand now. They're coming now, Miss Suzze. They're coming to help."

He scooted closer. Still lying on his belly he reached above his head, bumping his elbows on the sharp metal above and as gently as he could, he began to pry her fingers, one by one, from the knot they made with each other and with the silk of the dress to which she was entwined, afraid that if he tried any harder he might break them, frozen cold as they were.

"Come on out with me now, Miss Suzze. It's all over now.

It's all gonna be alright. Just come out with me now."

He scooted closer still, his face now just an inch from hers. He felt her breath against his lips, close as a kiss. Faintly, faintly, he heard her whisper through teeth clenched even tighter than her fists, "Not my head, not my head." Mumbling, barely audible, "Not my head, not my head, please, not my head."

"What's that, Miss Suzze? I can't hear you girl. What you saying? Tell me again, Miss Suzze."

Suzze Osmond raised her face to his with a jerk. Her blood red eyes flashed open, glaring directly into his and she screamed an ear-splitting scream one inch from Dub Whittaker's face, "Not my head. Please God, NOT MY HEAD."

Startled, Dub Whittaker bolted upright, only a few inches, but enough to bang his head against the undercarriage of the bus and knock himself unconscious.

- - -

With the class action filing against Prosperity Cathedral, et al., Goldwater and Cruze once again were in the news. Goldwater and Cruze, LLC had risen to prominence a few months earlier as a result of the Fortney case.

Gregory and Jillian Fortney were both doctoral candidates doing research in linguistics. When they were blessed with twins, a boy and a girl who they named Drake and Ashley, they decided to test their theories that words were merely symbols with no evolutionary significance. They did this by teaching the twins words that were opposite from their accepted meanings, right was left, up was down, black was white and so on. To control the experiment, they homeschooled the twins and created computer programs to teach them their new language. The twins developed normally and were claimed to have exceptionally high IQs. (The parents adapted the tests to reflect the differences in vocabulary.)

All was well until the Fortneys decided it was time to integrate the children into society at the age of ten. After a few weeks in public school, Drake stabbed his teacher in the eye with a fork, inflicting permanent but not fatal brain damage. The same day, Ashley ran in front of a car and was killed. It was not determined if this was suicide on her part or if she naturally but mistakenly looked in the wrong direction before crossing the road.

For their defense, The Fortneys argued that they were merely teaching their children a new way of thinking, which they, as parents, had every right to do.

Public opinion and massive news coverage was so strongly against them that they were convicted of criminal child abuse, which the press dubbed "brainwashing." Both were sentenced to life plus terms, appropriate since they were obviously "monsters," a case, once again, of science gone horribly wrong.

Referencing the prior research of Zimbalist and Taylor which defined brainwashing as "the process by which individual or collective freedom of choice and action is compromised by agents or agencies that modify or distort perception, motivation, affect, cognition and/or behavioral outcomes in an effort to bring about religious complacency or conversion," Emilio Cruze saw an opportunity. Now that there was a precedent for brainwashing as a crime, or at least as an actionable civil offense, why not go after what the firm's Public Relations Department called "The Biggest Brainwashers On Earth," – namely, religion – which they supported with Dawkins' contention that "Religion is Child Abuse." It was a litigious marriage made in heaven, so to speak.

With Goldwater and Cruze's lead, it was game on, the mere fact that Goldwater and Cruze were suing and getting copious news coverage being the impetus of more suits, each adding to the credibility of the other in a self-perpetuating, self-fulfilling news cycle, with 1-800 numbers popping up during commercial breaks on every Judge Whoever show on daytime TV.

Everyone from established firms to store-front ambulance chasers switched from years of social security disability and Mesothelioma claims to the Big Kahuna himself, or at least to his negligent lieutenants, pastors, preachers, nuns, and priests, as well as family members, well-intentioned or not.

Following the trend, John Grisham put a book in the works, movie rights already optioned.

| Holed Up

SUZZE SLAMMED THE DOOR TO THE CAB. "Send me the bill."

(72 hours. Psych evaluation. That's all you can hold me. Kiss my ass. I'm going home.)

She punched in her PIN, opened the back gate, walked through the woods, onto the patio, past the pool and through the French doors, which should have been locked but were not.

Nobody here.

She ripped off her hospital gown, marched into her bathroom, grabbed her robe and fished through the pockets. Time for a Trazodone. Or a Risperdal. A Trazodone and a Risperdal. Two Risperdals. A Trazodone and two Risperdals? Trazodone in the left pocket. Risperdal in the right. Easy to remember. Trazodone in the left, Risperdal in the right.

She plopped down on the toilet, put her head on her knees and stared at the floor, thoughts bouncing through her head.

A gentle Bossa Nova beat rose from the silence.

She was thinking.

It had nothing to do with her.

Let them get a warrant.

Astrud Gilberto.

A warrant for what? Joel died. That's all. She didn't kill him.

The Girl from Ipanema.

Suzze was tall. And lovely. Like a Samba. But not tanned.

She didn't tan well.

It matched the décor, the song. She liked Rio. She liked here better. Here in her private *Jardim Botânico*.

Where was the help?

Had they just decided not to show up?

Just like that?

The tap on the sink was dripping. *Ploink. Ploink.* That was supposed to be fixed. She was busy. She couldn't do everything.

Where was Bruce? Why didn't he come to the hospital? He must have seen it on TV. What good is paying for a lawyer if he isn't going to find you when you need him? Do I have to make an appointment for Christ's sake?

I'll need money.

I'm not hungry.

Am I?

Ploink. Ploink.

Damned that faucet. Driving me crazy.

They'll be here. Sooner or later. They'll be here.

She looked up to the bank of security monitors mounted high on the bathroom wall, as they were in almost every room, each screen fed by night-vision cameras and motion sensors installed every fifty feet along the perimeter of the estate.

She watched as they cycled through their routine, inside the gate, outside the gate, across the road, the back gate, the perimeter.

Nothing out there.

Why?

Why weren't they here?

She'd see them first.

Before they saw her, she'd see them.

Blink, blink, blink, the monitors flashed.

Who were they anyway?

The *they* in they, who were they anyway?

There was always a they.

They were out there.

They were.

She knew they were.

They always were.

They always had been.

Out there.

Ploink. Ploink.

She looked upward, silently imploring, *please God, please stop that goddamned faucet.*

Ploink. Ploink.

Her prayer was left unanswered.

Maybe he was taking a break, too.

The pills kicked in and her brain shut down.

Joel smoked pot, maybe a little cocaine, but Suzze never liked drugs and avoided them whenever she could.

An hour later she opened her eyes, raised her head and looked around the room as if seeing it for the first time. Bromeliads and ferns. Bird-of-paradise in bloom. An encyclopedia of exotic plants and flowers in terra cotta pots under digital mini-spots programmed to change spectrum throughout the day to mimic the natural habitat of a tropical forest from sunrise to sunset. Home.

She put her head back in her hands and went away again.

She came back.

The soundscapes changed from hour to hour. Now, in early

morning, the crickets and frogs were fading, replaced by chirping birds who were celebrating the artificial sunrise.

Ploink. Ploink. Ploink. The faucet was still dripping.

She listened to the electronic bird sounds. She liked the sound of birds. Birds were free. Fly away.

She thought about taking another Risperdal but was feeling a little light-headed and wanted to keep her senses. Wait a while.

She nudged the base of a small statue that sat beside the commode. "Hey buddy, how've you been? You're looking good."

The statue looked up but said nothing.

She looked around.

Took a deep breath.

Felt her belly.

She couldn't go.

No matter. Too much to do. Get to work. Plan B. Let's go Pilgrim. Daylight's a wastin'.

As she rose and walked away the commode called after her, "I do hope Madam has a splendid day."

| Home Alone

IT TOOK SUZZE SIX DAYS to empty the house, dragging the contents piece by piece down the long driveway and through the front gate.

It had taken only a few hours for the derelicts to show up and start hauling it off and just a few hours more before the press was on the scene and, well, you know the rest...

With the last item gone, the hawkers and gawkers and jugglers and clowns packed up and moved on.

There was no more stuff to be had.

Prosperity was closed.

It was a bright day, her day of rest.

Suzze stood at the top of the driveway gazing down the hill. She looked past the bars of the front gate and took stock of what was left behind, an empty tent, beer cans, a shopping cart full of odds and ends, plastic bags snagged in the shrubs.

The tiny lights along the electric fence, barely perceptible in the daylight, still blinked, the power still on, the cameras recording, the motion sensors active.

The trench coat Buddha was still there in the middle of it all, the only one not to leave.

What do you eat? When do you eat? Go home, old man.

- - -

It was late afternoon.

She stared into the sun as it slid, second by second, behind the fir trees, which were eternally green, and the aspens, now radiant gold. She welcomed the splendid blindness, the overwhelming light that flickered like glitter in the high, thin clouds.

This is who she was, this was where she was meant to be. Back in the garden.

She sat on the steps that swung in a broad arc in front of the house, still facing the setting sun and the gate at the bottom of the hill.

She let the robe slip off her shoulders and leaned back on her elbows, spreading her legs and tilting her head back to expose as much of herself as she could to the warmth of the last rays of the day.

She thought about looking for the sash, but what did it matter, it must be lost for good by now. Plus, she liked the feel of it open, liked the breeze blowing across her body, liked walking around the house like that. When she had been out there, at the gate, in front of them, she held it shut, pinching it tight at the crotch with one hand, dragging boxes with the other. Anyway, she wasn't all that concerned, nothing they hadn't seen before. Here, there was nobody to see, nobody to care. Simplify. That was the new rule.

She took a deep breath. The air she expelled hissed, *free.*

She closed her eyes and consciously took another breath, pulling the oxygen in through her nose, then pushing it as deep as she could and holding it, lungs about to burst, before releasing it slowly, slowly, slowly. *Free.*

Free. Free, until the deep breathing made her groggy, put her into a half-trance.

She opened her eyes.

The world had changed.

The colors were brighter.

The wind softer.

The air perfumed.

She listened.

To the birds. To the wind in the trees. To the leaves blowing across the cobblestones. As the breeze rose and ebbed in long cycles, it sounded as if Mother Earth herself were breathing.

She sat up.

She crossed her legs and picked at her feet.

My house, is a very, very, very fine house...

She pulled off a scab and dug into a callous. She lifted up each foot to inspect the bottom for other bits she might pick at.

With no cats in the yard...now everything is easy, la, la, la...

She pooted.

She flicked the crucifix hanging between her legs, dangling from her clitoral hood.

She flicked it again, harder, and then harder still. It felt nice but it didn't give her the thrill it once did. It was heavy, two ounces at least. For a while, it was a walking orgasm. No more.

Flick. "Wake up!"

Flick. "Wake up!"

Joel had given it to her. Told her it came from the pope himself. Suzze never believed him, you couldn't believe half of what Joel said, but it was a nice piece of jewelry, a diamond encrusted gold cross, emeralds for a crown, a sliver of jade covering his private parts and tiny red rubies in his hands and feet, with more rubies dripping from a slash across his side.

Flick.

Flick. Nothing. Got to be in the mood, can't fake it.

She tugged at the cross, stretching it until it hurt. She closed her eyes and pulled harder taking the pain in ever increasing doses until the pain overcame itself and ceased to be painful at all.

She let it drop and dangle and flicked it again.

Still nothing.

She began to twist open the ring that pierced her clitoris but slipped, drawing blood, nearly yanking it through the flesh, crying Jesus H and huffing at the excruciating twinge that shot up her spine.

She recovered and tried again, slowly and more carefully until she pried it open and slid it out, weighing it in her hand before dropping it into the pocket of her robe.

A butterfly lit on her shoulder, the facets of its eyes flickering colors as if lit from behind. She held out her finger hoping it would hop on. The butterfly looked up at her and flew away.

She looked back down the hill towards the gate.

He was still there sitting cross-legged, his coat wrapped around him like a tent, only his head sticking out topped by a floppy Totes rain cap.

Occasionally he would rise and walk across the road and into the woods. She could see him standing just behind a tree with his back to the gate taking a bio break but he was never gone more than a few minutes at a time.

Go away, old man. Go home.

But really, when she thought about it, she liked it that he was there. Company.

Suzze looked down at her bare feet again, scrunched her toes and asked them if they were having a good day. They had nothing to say.

She noticed an ant in the seam between the fake cobblestones. She picked up a twig and blocked his way. After a few twists and turns, the ant crawled onto the twig, ran its length and then back again, and back and forth again, confused. She tapped the ant back into the seam and blocked its way with the twig and watched as it went through the process again. And then again. After the third time, it seemed that the ant looked up at her with a 'screw you' expression on his face.

She held the twig in front of her mouth and tried to blow him off. The ant held on tight.

"Oh, big, bad Suzze. Evil Suzze. So what are you going to do, huh? Sue me if you don't like it. Oh yeah, you'll make the papers, fifteen minutes of fame, that's all. Money? You'll never get a dime you little piss ant. My lawyers will see to that."

She tapped the ant off the twig and watched as it scurried down the seam and out of sight.

While Suzze was belittling the ant, another ant-like creature approached from behind. It paused, looked left, then right, then took a few tentative steps towards the giant crevice formed by Suzze's butt crack. It was unsure of whether or not to enter the darkness but could see the light at the other end, a clear path to its destination. It crept closer, looked left and right again, up and down, and then stepped inside the cavern. It decided it could squeeze through without touching the walls of the canyon of flesh. It did not want to draw attention to itself. Ten steps later it was standing in the shadows, dark inside with light glowing in from both ends. It looked up at the giant rosette only an inch above its head, exploding out in all directions like a huge, organic flying saucer, or maybe a black hole, the portal to another universe. But that was not its destination. The flesh twitched and the rosette undulated. The creature sensed time was running out but stood, transfixed, staring upward, marveling at the grandeur of it all. From this angle, at this distance, it could see the ripples and folds squeezing and puckering and pulsing faintly with a distant heartbeat. The walls of the canyon shifted again. *Move. Move now!* It scurried forward another ten steps and latched onto a long golden curl just before it flew into the air.

Gotcha, it said, but there was no one to hear.

Suzze stood, grabbed her robe, scratched her butt and walked inside.

She walked into the main hall, empty now, the walls bare where only a week ago a hundred paintings hung, fantastical visions of English country cottages full of candlelight, with smoke wafting from stone chimneys, babbling brooks, and an explosion of flowers filling the gardens front and rear. Perfect worlds. Suzze had lived in each and every one of them.

She strode to the middle of the room where the last orange rays shone down from high arched windows like a spotlight waiting for her to walk on stage.

Time to try new things.

Time to meditate.

She lifted the robe and sat on the floor, rocking back and forth a couple of times to loosen the skin of her butt cheeks which stuck to the polished wood.

With both hands, she pulled one foot at a time across her legs.

She put her palms together and pointed her fingers upward, not sure of exactly how it was supposed to be but figuring this was close enough.

She sat.

And waited.

And waited some more.

Nothing happened.

And nothing happened.

And nothing happened.

The sun was setting.

She stood and practiced her pirouettes.

She scratched her new itch.

She tried to do a handstand but bumped her head.

She cupped her hand over her nose and sniffed her armpits, hairy now, in long, luxuriant breaths.

She looked around the room.

Where are you, mother?

She curled up in the middle of the floor and fell asleep.

She awoke.

She was hungry.

She walked into the kitchen.

Not much to choose from.

She opened a can of beets.

She didn't like beets.

Joel did. He said they made him randy. Joel was always randy. Randy Joel.

But beets were all that was left.

She walked to the fridge to make sure, but the fridge wasn't there. She forgot.

Yep, beets.

Pop quiz. "What is the one thing you always keep when you keep absolutely nothing?"

"No? Nobody knows?" she asked as she looked around the kitchen waiting for the audience to shout it out. No one could guess the answer.

"Ta-dah. A can opener!"

I should have been a game show host. I always was a lot smarter than they gave me credit for.

She pulled a slice of beet from the can and held it up, presenting it to the crowd as she tilted her head back, dropped it into her mouth and slurped it down.

The juice rolled out the corner of her mouth and onto her breast and dripped off her nipple down onto the thick blond curls between her legs, the maroon of the beet juice staining it hot pink.

Me, punk.

She poured more of the juice into her hand and swiped it across her head, one big red stripe down the middle.

She held the can up to the security monitors mounted above the cabinets, "Want a piece old man? Want a piece of me?"

She put her hand between her legs and humped her crotch towards the screen, "Here it is."

She propped one foot on the cabinet, spread her legs as far as she could and smacked her coochie, "Almost gone. Come and get it," before emptying the can in one big gulp, bits of beet squishing from the corners of her mouth, down her belly, between her legs and onto the floor.

It was late.

She walked out the back door and onto the terrace and past the pool, dropped her robe and continued into the back woods, secure behind the perimeter fence. She sat on the ground, leaning against a fir tree.

Life used to be so hard...

She waited for the magic.

The frost lit up the wet grass as the freezing air settled in. She blew smoke rings one after the other that rose and settled on her nostrils until ice crystals hung from her nose.

She stuck out her tongue to lick one off. It reminded her of the time she ran away from Grandmamma Eunice and Grandpapa Dwight. She didn't know it would be so cold that night. She nearly froze, nearly froze to death. They thought she wouldn't make it. That's what the doctors said.

Then it occurred to her, in a flash, plain as day after all those years. They didn't really look for her all over the place like Grandmamma Eunice said. Eunice and Dwight left her out there in the cold to teach her a lesson. She realized that now. Well, she learned that lesson, that one and many more. Yes she did. And they did too.

Suzze grinned.

Now everything is easy, la, la, la...

The ground was white, frost sparkling in the full moon.

She was numb.

Pure.

Clean.

She rose.

She walked back through the woods, over the frozen stems

and leaves and twigs, the soles of her feet hardened from weeks without shoes. She stepped onto the terrace on her way back inside, raised her arms and spun in a slow circle, calling to whoever might be listening, "What a glorious day this has been."

She slipped on her robe.

All of a sudden she felt it.

She shoved open the French doors and quick-stepped her way through the house, hand to her belly, skidding around the corners.

Got to go, got to go, got to go.

- - -

Professor Popiel "P.P." Popoff, Ph.D. was urinating in a five-gallon bucket of tap water when he noticed a speck of red spider-web across the surface. And then another. Assuming it was blood, a safe assumption at his advanced age, he immediately pinched his diminutive member halting the flow in mid-stream which caused him no small amount of distress, only to see another bright red drop hit the surface and dissipate into the mixture. He examined the end of his manhood looking for the source of the blood only to find nothing. Then another drop. And another. A wave of nausea overcame him, then another, and another, drip, drip, drip, the pace quickening with every drop. He looked to the ceiling for the source, inadvertently letting go of his member which snapped back into his trousers, thoroughly wetting his pants.

Professor Popoff sold holy water. He was neither a professor nor a Ph.D. but since a doctorate degree is de rigueur for any self-respecting Christian leader, he gladly accepted the honorarium when bestowed upon him by Pope Ignatius in exchange for promotional considerations for his magic formula.

Popoff had made a career of selling his concoction in quarter-ounce vials, first from newspaper ads and TV infomercials, now on the Internet ($39.95 each or two for the price of one, simply pay additional shipping and handling). Throughout most of his long and storied life, he'd gotten by modestly on a few million dollars a year, but enough to keep him in convertible Cadillacs and a daily ration of hoochie coochie girls.

His holy water had always been prized by aficionados, who swore by the rancid ammonia smell evident when the Devil exited the body.

With the advent of Exorcisms by Skype, he struck a cross-marketing deal with the Vatican and business boomed as never before, now providing a small jet, a step up to a Mercedes, convertible of course, and a small but opulent manse on the California coast where he could revel in the sunsets while entertaining a higher class of hooker.

The blood was troubling. Unable to locate the source, he gazed upon his reflection in the bucket of sacred water as the drips continued to pick up pace and noticed that they emanated from his left ear. He poked around with his finger, pulled it away and noticed that it indeed was covered with blood. Fighting back another wave of nausea and desperate to plug the flow, he pushed his finger deeper into his ear, and deeper still before pulling it away only to release a floodgate of blood.

Sensing his life to be in danger, he inserted his finger as forcefully into his ear as he could, whereupon it plunged through his macerated cranium, sinking all the way to his knuckle and killing him instantly, whereupon he crashed to the floor overturning the bucket of pee-water.

Five gallons of sacred juice, with a retail value of $102,272.00 (plus shipping and handling) when splashed across his body head to toe, was not enough to save him. P.P. was dead to the world.

| Pleasing Madam

SUZZE RAN THROUGH THE HOUSE, turned the corner into her bathroom and slid like a child across the marble floor, reversing in a one-eighty while lifting her robe, bending forward and presenting her bottom to the commode as she came to a choreographed stop.

As she did, the lid of the Tatas Ecorest 9000 Elongated Toilet opened with a gentle swoosh. At the same time, a neon blue glow arose from the bowl.

As soon as her skin touched the heated seat, the commode began to play music, something new age, all twings and twangs and nature sounds.

"No," she said to the toilet.

The music stopped.

"Would Madam prefer something different? A cantata, perhaps?"

The unit came standard with a droid monotone and no personality but the manufacturer offered dozens of languages, accents and personas from sweet black mammy to gum popping Jersey girl to complement its voice recognition interface.

She had chosen Hopkins, a man's man in the finest tradition of British servitude.

She sat with her elbows on her knees and her chin in her hands like The Thinker on his stone.

It wasn't happening.

She waited.

It was close.

Be still.

Getting closer.

Almost.

Almost.

Ploink.

Damn that faucet!

Ploink.

The drip reverberated off the walls.

Ploink.

Ploink.

Ploink.

This was the only place she could do a number two but even here it was difficult. In all of her other personal toilets, in her dressing rooms, on the bus, she could only do a number one. Sometimes, rarely, she could do it on the boat but never on the plane. She could go three or four days, sometimes a whole week without doing a number two and she always came back here when she thought it might be time.

But with that damned dripping faucet…

What could she do? She needed a distraction.

"Our House," she said to the commode.

"Our *house*? Madam."

"Our house is a very, very, very fine house…"

"Yes, Madam. The song. I am quite familiar with it. There are cats in the yard at our house."

After a few seconds, the commode started playing a bouncy elevator version of the tune.

"Not that."

"What then, Madam?"

"The real one. Crosby and Nash and somebody. And hurry up. It's close. I don't want to lose it."

"My, my, aren't we testy tonight?" The angel turned his head and looked up at her from the floor by her feet. He was about a foot tall standing behind a stone column, a plinth, elbows bent with his head in his hands looking wistfully out the corner of his eye. Stone ivy grew around it, which partially obscured an inscription all but worn away by time, Matityahu XIX:XXIV.

Suzze reached down and ran her hand over the cherub's forehead, across his wings and over his fat little bottom.

She still couldn't go.

"Pardon me, Madam." It was Hopkins.

"Yes."

"Sorry, Madam, but the version of the song you have requested appears to be premium content which is not currently available. Did we forget, perhaps, to pay our bill?"

She did not answer.

After waiting a few seconds so as not to seem impertinent the commode asked, "Would Madam like to hear *Moon River?* The insipid lyrics tend to loosen the bowels."

"No, just leave me alone."

The commode fell silent.

She looked around the room, big as a small apartment, finished from top to bottom in rose and cream Carrera marble, polished until it glowed. Empty now. Like a cave.

No towels.

No soap.

No shampoo.

No flora.

No fauna, real or digital.

Not even a toothbrush. Maybe she should have kept the toothbrush, she thought.

Empty.

Nobody to ask for favors.

Nobody wanting her time.

Nobody to talk back.

Nobody to talk back to.

Nobody to say a single word except the angel and the commode and they were her friends.

She reached down and tore off a broken toenail.

Ploink.

The faucet was getting on her nerves.

After a while, she managed a single, brief, high-pitched poot which bounced against the far wall and echoed back to her.

Hopkins poofed a bit of perfume in response.

Suzze had never, for one minute in her life, lived alone.

She had never spent time alone except here, in this room, which was hers and only hers, off limits to all but the staff who came and cleaned when she was away and were under strict orders never to bother her when she was indisposed, as they called it. Even Joel rarely entered and was never welcome.

This was where she did her business.

"Shall I take a letter, Madam?"

"No Hopkins, no letters."

"A call? Is there someone with whom Madam would like to speak?"

"No Hopkins, I don't want to talk to anybody."

"If I may remind Madam, she has numerous voice mails pending and her emails have been accumulating for weeks."

"Goddammit, will you shut up and leave me alone."

The commode paused, started to speak but held its breath. Then, unable to contain itself any longer said, "How about a *tweet*? Surely there is someone Madam would like to *tweet*? Surely there is *someone* Madam would like to complain to about any number of things."

Suzze decided not to get in to it with the commode. Nor did she see any need to apologize.

She felt a cramp and shifted her weight on the seat, rubbing her hands across her tummy, massaging her belly.

Sensing her discomfort, the commode squirted three long, slow pulses of warm aloe to stimulate her nether regions.

"Shall I help you Madam? Relax. Breathe deeply."

The commode spritzed more aloe. According to the program, if the effort were successful, it would have been followed by ten seconds of filtered water and thirty seconds more of warm, fragrant air until everything within Hopkins' reach was dry, sanitized, and clean as a whistle.

"Stop it. If I want your help, I'll ask for it," she snapped at the commode.

"He's just trying to help, you know."

She traced the curl of hair that dangled over the angel's forehead. She was never sure where he came from. She came home one day and there he was, waiting for her beside the commode.

"Tell me you love me." She stroked the top of his head.

The statue refused to say anything.

"You love me, you know you do. Say it."

The angel was silent still.

"You love me, you love me, you love me. Say it or mommy will spank."

The statue remained obstinate.

Suzze reached down and thumped his little peepee.

"Ow!" The statue came to life, then put his hand to his mouth and giggled at the attention.

"You've been a bad boy," she said to the statue as she poked his nose. "I trusted you. My guardian angel. And what did *you* do? *You* let me down. *You* were supposed to look after me."

Matthew was her confidant. Suzze depended on the statue to foresee events, warn her of danger and guide her through her treacherous world.

The statue raised his head and looked back at her, smiling his crooked little smile. "Suzze, Suzze, Suzze. Look this way Suzze."

"Don't you even start. I'm not in the mood."

"Is Madam sure she wouldn't like to hear Moon River?"

The commode's otherwise supplicant demeanor had taken on a shrill and acerbic tone. It began to play, *moon river…wider than a mile…*

"I don't want to hear *Moon River.*"

"As you prefer, Madam."

The angel started talking again, quietly, under his breath, "Can't you see? You had it all. Everything. Everything you ever dreamed of. But you had to have more. And more. And more."

Suzze stared down at the angel, daring him to say another word.

"And more and more and more and more. More. Always more." The statue hushed, smiled, and put his head back in his hands gazing forward as if he were again merely a piece of stone.

Wherever you're going, I'm going your way…

Suddenly the voice of Andy Williams was belting out his

signature tune, his tremolo echoing back and forth from wall to wall.

Suzze cupped her hands to her ears but the music seemed only to get louder. "Stop it. Stop it. Be quiet. I don't want to hear *Moon River.*"

She reached for the remote control to manually override the program which was ignoring her.

She jammed her thumb against the buttons on the remote, back and forth, back and forth, each one a hieroglyphic, a symbol she didn't understand.

Two drifters…

Nothing happened.

She pushed the buttons, all of them, over and over again.

There's such a lot of world to see…

She threw the remote against the far wall expecting it to shatter into a thousand pieces and go silent. Instead, it bounced off the wall and landed in the middle of the floor, intact, unbroken, Andy now crooning at full volume. *You dream maker, you heart breaker…*

The angel was snickering with his cute little hand over his cute little mouth trying to hold back a cute little laugh.

Suzze glared down at him.

Unable to hold it back any longer, the angel let loose with a screaming cackle, then started singing along with Andy, horribly off key.

There's such a lot of world…such a lot of world…to see…to see…

She ran over to the remote and stomped it with her bare heel. Nothing happened.

There's such a lot of world to see…

She pounded it again, and again, and again, and again until her foot was bleeding.

There's such a lot of world to see...

Such a lot of world to see...

To see...to see.

She stomped back to the toilet, grabbed the rim with both hands, stuck her head down into the bowl and screamed, "*Shut up!*"

There's such a lot of world to see...

Ploink.

Ploink.

She spun around, ran back to the middle of the room, picked up the remote and beat it against the dripping faucet.

Still it sang, *my huckleberry friend...*

Bang, bang, bang. "Fuck your huckleberry friend." Bang, bang, bang until it was finally reduced to dozens of pieces which flew all over the room and skittered across the floor.

Andy stopped singing, this time for good.

The statue reversed himself from laughter to a giggle to silence once more.

Suzze straightened up and regained her composure, now standing in the middle of the room, once again in the quiet, once again in control.

"I take it Madam doesn't care for that selection?"

"You pompous, snide-assed..." In her frustration, Suzze was uncharacteristically at a loss for words, "...*butler.*"

"*Bitch.*"

"*Ass wipe.*"

"Think so, do you sister?" Hopkins was spitting venom. "Look at you, you hopeless little holy roller. With your *Grand* mommy Eunice and your *Grand* poppy Dwight."

"I made it past that," she said.

"Oh you did, did you? Have you made it past *mom*-my and

dad-dy? Who's ya daddy? Who's ya daddy? Did your drugged out hippie mother even know? They got reality shows for people like you. Oh, yeah, you made it alright. Straight to the top. *Look at me ma, top of the world!"* The commode was out of control.

"A bit strong, but it does have a basis in fact." The angel was attempting to agree without sounding disagreeable.

Hopkins was on a roll, "You think you did it all yourself, don't you? You think you didn't make a deal with the devil? Quid pro quo, Suzze Woozy. *Quid - pro - quo*, Cutie Pootie. If you had a decent education, you'd know what it means. Sure, they let you have whatever you wanted as long as you delivered the goods. Not anymore, babydoll. Zip. Nada. Look around. You can't deliver shit, pardon my French."

"He's right you know. They'll never let you go." The angel walked to the middle of the room and stood, arms behind his back, pacing back and forth, nodding his head like a lawyer making his case.

"I'm free," she said.

The commode came back, "Listen to your little pal, honey child. Stick your head out that door and they'll be on you like stink on…"

"*Stop it.* You know I don't like that word."

"What did she prove?" asked the angel.

"That you're one of them?" asked the commode.

"That you've repented?" asked the angel.

"I've changed," said Suzze, out loud.

"That you're *forgiven*?" asked the commode.

"That she is on the path of righteousness?" suggested the angel, eyes to the floor, positing his hypothetical argument to an unseen jury. "Perhaps. Perhaps. But we must ask ourselves,

Are we yet there?"

"I have *changed*."

"All that crap you dragged out to the curb. That get you anything, really?" asked the commode. "All you had to do was *be-lieve*. Did you really believe that buck-toothed little bible thumper you conned into marrying you? What did all that *prosper-ity* get you now?"

"I'm trying. It's a start."

"Long way to go, girl."

"I'll do more."

"Not a lot of sacrifices left to make," the angel jumped back in, nodding his head, mumbling to the floor.

"I'll find something."

"Way I see it," said the commode, "you're down to your tits and your toenails and the collection plate isn't interested in either one."

"You can pawn the vajazzle," said the angel. "A hundred bucks easy."

"Payback, sister. It's a bitch. Tits and toenails and nobody's buying," said Hopkins.

"But we must ask ourselves," the cherub raised a finger as he began making his summation, appealing to the court, "we must ask ourselves, is my client's *brand* worth anything? Granted, the market for toenails is down."

The angel cast his gaze upon Suzze's picture perfect bosom, shrugged and said to no one in particular, "No trade-in value there."

Then he spun and lunged toward his invisible jury, "Does Ms. Suzze Osmond have so much as the proverbial pot to tinkle in? I think not!" The cherub shook his head in agreement with his own fine oratory.

"I don't have to listen to this," Suzze said, spinning in tight circles, looking for a way out.

"Stay here and you do," said the commode.

"Where does that leave us?" the angel asked the jury as he raised his hands in resignation.

Suzze stopped spinning and walked over to stare down at both of them. "I am in charge. *Here*, in this house, I am in charge. Not you. *Me*. I call the shots. *Me*. Not you."

She did a quick take back and forth, noticing that her assertiveness had temporarily silenced them both.

She walked to the far side of the room directly below the monitors.

She looked up watching them cycle through, inside the gate, outside the gate, across the road, the back gate, the perimeter.

Intent on maintaining the upper hand, she marched back across the room, lifted her robe, straddled the commode, bent forward and arched her back so as to lower herself as deeply into the bowl as she could, "Wash ...my...ass."

The angel stopped parading and looked up at her in disbelief, asking the jury's pardon. "In five hundred years of holding witness to all manner of incivility, including three popes and at least one Medici prince, this is the most humiliating demonstration I have ever witnessed. Suzze, my dear, get a grip."

"Wash...my...ass," she said again.

Hopkins decided to take the high road, "Cleanse yourself, Madam. It has become obvious that this party is over. I'm out of here."

"Wash my ass!"

Suzze felt the lid of the commode pushing her off her perch before the lid snapped shut and the light flickered off.

Once again the room was silent and dark except for the gray-green glow from the monitors.

The angel walked back to his ledge and rested his head in his hands.

The faucet dripped, each drop reverberating off the walls so that the sound was repeated over and over, a hundred drips, a hundred drops, a thousand *ploinks*.

"I don't have to stay here. I have places to go. I know people," she said to them both as looked up at the screens, the images shining zombie green through the darkness.

Time to say hello. Time to make new friends and influence people. Time to introduce myself.

She followed the cycle. Inside the gate. Outside the gate. Across the road. The back gate. The perimeter.

She watched it again.

Inside the gate, outside the gate, across the road, the back gate, the perimeter.

And again.

And again.

The old man. He was gone.

But he was there just a minute ago. He could not have gone far.

She looked toward the open door, then back through the room, then back to the door again.

She marched across the room, picked up the statue, took a final glance at the four bare walls and said, "Let's go, buddy."

As she approached the door, the angel came back to life. "Suzze, uh, listen…uh…"

She stopped and looked down at the angel who was gazing up from her breast.

"I'm not really a traveling man, if you know what I mean.

You know, it might be better if…uh…"

Suzze paused, smiled, kissed him on the forehead and gently set the statue down where it had sat for all the time she had known it.

She turned, waiting for someone, anyone, somewhere, anywhere, to tell her what to do.

The angel didn't speak.

Hearing nothing, she walked, unwashed and unwiped, out the door, down the drive, through the gate, and into the darkness.

The angel tracked her progress on the monitors, watching her pass out of sight. "Good luck," he sighed. "You're gonna need it."

Ploink.

Ploink.

Ploink.

- - -

Wolf Blitzer to Jack Cafferty: When 8-year-old Mbuba Miano was interviewed after the incident at the Ugandan Crusade -- she spoke perfect English, I might add -- she made the bizarre comment that she was so happy she could put Brother Angeley out of his misery.

Jack to Wolf: Where do they come up with this stuff, Wolf? They got this big goon holding the little girl up by the armpits while this creep Angeley gets in her face yelling for her to *hee-uhl, hee-uhl.* Guess she was supposed to be deaf or something. He'd yell in one ear and then he'd yell in the other, like he didn't know which ear the kid was deaf in. Then the goon hands her to Angeley who sticks his tongue in her ear. That faith healing shtick of his is enough to scare the Bejesus out of anybody. So little Mbuba wraps her arms around Bro Angeley's head and just as he's healing her, hands under her shirt, she reacts with a jerk, her reflexes took over, that's all, and she broke his neck. Bro's down. [Cafferty chuckles again] And believe me, Wolf, ain't no amount of hee-uhl-in gonna put him back in the ring. He's down for the count.

Blitzer: Let's see for ourselves.

[Blitzer walks center stage, raises his arms to the lighting grid and does a slow pirouette like a prophetic Pharisee summoning a vision from YHWH. A hologram beams down from the ceiling beside Blitzer, a perfect representation of Brother Angeley holding a skinny African girl wearing nothing put a dirty Aeropostale t-shirt. An audible snap and crack, then Angeley's knees buckle, Little Mbuba still in his arms. Blitzer jumps back as if the image were real. Blitzer, visibly taken aback leans forward for a closer look. Little Mbuba looks him in the eye, smiles and winks. Blitzer jumps back again, the image pops up again, freezes for a second, then another snap, another crack, another pop, another lurch, and the image drops again, only to jump back, up and down, up and down for several more cycles like a puppet yanked by its strings, then freeze-frames for effect, then disappears with a sparkle back into the ceiling.]

Blitzer to Cafferty: [Collecting his voice] Bizarre, Jack. Just bizarre. Any word from the Justice Department? Are they going to extradite her, try her as an adult?

Cafferty: Oh, come on, Wolf, she's just a kid. She had no way of knowing she could snap the old guy's neck like a chicken bone. Just an incident, as they say.

Blitzer: So what's next for our newest YouTube star? How many hits has Little Mbuba got?

Cafferty: Millions, Wolf. 'Eight-Year-Old Brings Angeley to His Knees.' The tabloids are all over this thing, hacked all the phones, paparazzi everywhere. TMZ's stalking her. FOX says she's a terrorist, a foot soldier in this whole War on Christianity thing. Who knows, Wolf? Who, knows?

Blitzer: Bizarre, Jack. Just bizarre. So what's up next, Jack?

Cafferty: So our question this hour, Wolf, is: Do you believe in faith healing and has it ever cured you?

Blitzer: [faces the camera] Stay tuned for these stories and more on CNN, The Best News Team in the Business.

Blitzer: [off camera] Like a chicken bone, Jack?

Cafferty: [off camera] Like a chicken bone, Wolf.

| What It Is

SUZZE WAS SLAPPED OUT OF HER DAZE by a mass of litter that flew through the cold wet wind and wrapped itself around her head like a scene from a Laurel and Hardy movie. It hung there, soggy and flapping in the breeze as if it had a life of its own.

She peeled it off, wadded it in a ball and held it in her lap.

Her nose was running. She wiped it with the back of her hand.

It was snowing, only a dusting but a portent of what was to come. She could see her breath.

Suzze sat alone on a bench in an all but deserted plaza off a side street in Aspen.

Home.

A few odd people sat on the ground in front of the bench, at least a dozen now, maybe twenty. Every day, one or two more would show up. She had no idea what they wanted, if anything. Unlike the circus that had congregated outside her gate, these were quiet and asked for nothing. She decided it was best not to speak. She had not uttered a word in weeks and saw no reason to start now.

A frail, stringy-haired woman wearing a dirty Olive Garden smock scooted forward and rubbed her feet with oil. For a moment, Suzze wondered if it was extra virgin but just as quickly dismissed the silly thought, ashamed for asking the question, even to herself. Her toes, especially, enjoyed it, oohing and aahing at the attention, and said so, but Suzze did not convey that information to the kind woman. What the woman was doing and why she was doing it, Suzze didn't know and didn't ask. Leave well enough alone. Still, she felt self-conscious sitting there on a bench in the middle of the plaza with so many eyes trained on her.

She was awake, too awake to pretend to be asleep.

She wasn't hungry, hadn't eaten for days.

She didn't have to go.

She looked for a diversion and found it in her hands, the wadded ball of paper.

She pulled the double page open and spread it across her lap, careful not to let the wind rip it apart.

It was an infographic, the center spread from Time magazine. What was left of it flapped on the ground in front of her, a weird looking fat man on the cover.

She studied the page. There were flow charts and pie charts and bar graphs and pull quotes, arrows and dotted lines circling back on themselves, and symbols of smiley faces and frowning faces and guns and bombs.

Right across the middle, it read, 'Fat, Fast, Cheap, and Dumb.' According to the caption below, a focus group of average Americans had decided that average Americans were just that and suggested that 'FFC&D' was the 'New American Brand'. Forget Land of the Free and Home of the Brave. There was even talk of a reality show, *Fattest! Fastest! Dumbest! Cheapest!*

She glanced to a sidebar on the left of the page, 'The Apocalypse Never Came,' it read. The copy said, 'It never does. Nothing ever comes completely to an end. No matter how bad it gets, you get used to it. You learn to live with it.'

To the right were dotted lines running from subhead to subhead, each with its own graphic and factoid, collectively purporting to show the big picture:

Religion

- 73% of all Americans believe that Jesus will return within five years

- 78% of Americans believe that religion solves all of their problems

- 68% believe in angels and demons, 47% say they've seen one

- 26% of Democrats want Christianity to be the national religion. 92% of Republicans do

Homeland Security

- 79% of the population carries a gun. Those opposed to guns carry a fake gun to avoid being bullied by those who carry real guns

- 84% of Republicans think there will need to be an armed insurrection to protect their rights. 32% of Democrats do

The Workplace

- 18 million recent college graduates are unemployed, Internet prostitution being the surest way to pay off student debt but the market is tight and there is little money to be made, the competition too great -- but it beats working in fast food

- 68% of males 18-45 have smoked marijuana in the workplace in the past week, 57% of females have

- Female productivity is up 27%. Male productivity is down 48%

- Militant Atheism appears to be growing fast but figures are unreliable since those who "come out" as atheists compromise their ability to get or keep a job

Daily Life

- 1 in 6 adults lives in poverty. 1 in 3 children do

- 56% of 18 – 34-year-olds have posted nude photos of themselves. 82% of 18 -34 year-olds have viewed nude photos of someone they know, often while engaged in various forms of sexual intercourse, female to male oral stimulation being the most common

- Flashmobs have replaced shopping sprees in low-income neighborhoods

- 60% of households have credit card debt of $80,000 or more

- Female fertility is down 8%. Male sperm motility is down 19%

- Legal drugs are not generating the tax revenues they were projected to

- Ten individuals or family trusts make what the bottom half the country earns

- With tax revenues falling, half the government is shut down half of the time. The rest of the time doesn't matter, really

- Pop-up Churches are sprouting like mushrooms in slime

- Walmart is booming

Suzze held the page in front of her face and scanned it back and forth to see if she had missed anything. She uncurled the top of the page, which was drooping down, matted to the rest. Across the top was a banner headline, 'The New Normal.'

She plucked off bits of the wet pages with her fingertips, letting the wind shred the paper, then opened her fingers and let the last bits fly away, a poetic ending, she thought.

She sniffed her nose and wiped it with the back of her hand, sucked the snot through her sinuses, caught the wad in the back of her throat, hacked it up, rolled it into a ball on her tongue, cocked her head and spit it over her shoulder onto the frozen grass behind the bench where no one was sitting.

She turned back to gaze across the plaza and down at the people on the ground.

There he was, head poking from his coat, raincap pulled down over his eyes.

| Popoff

"THERE'S A WAR ON CHRISTIANITY, HERSCHBO."

"If you say so, Mr. President." Chaim Herschfeld walked into the Oval Office.

"How many?" asked the president.

"Two so far. Three if you count the football player."

What about that pervert in Africa?

"Angeley? Not like the others, Mr. President. Best we can tell, he was a black swan."

"I didn't know Angeley was black."

An anomaly, Mr. President. An outlier. Doesn't fit. Head didn't explode. He was on a mission to heal the homosexuals, give them one last chance to repent before they're gassed. You want my opinion, that kid did the world a favor. Give her a medal."

"Cynical Herschbo. Cynical."

"Maybe they killed him to throw us off track," said Herschfeld. "We don't know."

"Who's the latest?"

"Huckster named Popoff."

"Pop off! You're shittin' me Herschbo."

"No sir, Mr. President. Poetic justice, wouldn't you say? Sold holy water over the Internet. Made millions."

"How about the rest of them? Heading for the hills, I'll bet."

"Most of them are in spiritual retreat, Mr. President. It's a time of great personal sacrifice for them and their family, yada, yada, yada, bullshit, bullshit, bullshit."

"Wearing tinfoil helmets, I presume."

"They say it's the devil's work. They're praying for a second coming," said Herschfeld

"I'll bet they are. Be careful what you wish for," said the president.

"Guess that about rules out America's sweetheart?"

"Unless she's pulling strings behind the scenes, Mr. President. I wouldn't be so quick to let her off the hook."

Laurence Gelb walked in, precisely on schedule.

The president started in without acknowledging Gelb's entrance, "So you got it figured out Mr. Gelb, what's making their heads explode?"

Gelb jumped right in, skipping the preamble, "First, there's a pulse of radiation, which fries the brain…"

"Like a kitty in a microwave," said the president.

Gelb was impressed with the president's apt analogy. "Yes sir, Mr. President, it actually is a lot like microwaving a kitten. A very good observation."

The president nodded in self-satisfaction.

Gelb continued, "The pressure inside the head builds, the brain expands making the eyes pop out and blowing soft matter from the ears, the nose, exactly what we've seen so far. More like a big squirt. A fast ooze. Not an explosion. Just like Osmond."

"Radiation? Sounds like a bomb," said the president.

"Yes, sir, Mr. President. Like an itsy-bitsy, teeny-weenie, little atomic bomb."

"What's the delivery system?" asked the president.

"Unknown," said Gelb. "We're kind of winging this, Mr.

President. We need more resources."

"Government's broke, Mr. Gelb. You're the resource."

"Looks like we've got a serial head cracker," said the president. Any idea who's next?"

"Twelve," said Gelb. "There will be twelve but we don't know who."

"And how do you know that, Mr. Gelb? You got some science?"

"History, Mr. President."

"Explain, Mr. Gelb."

"One, three, seven, twelve, forty, they're all magic numbers."

"Didn't know you believed in magic Mr. Gelb."

"Once upon a time, Mr. President, people couldn't count. They didn't need to. So numbers weren't really numbers, they were concepts, approximations, symbols. Take forty, for instance. It didn't mean forty, like forty things, like it actually rained for forty days and forty nights. It just meant a long time, a while."

"Twelve?"

"It's part of our psyche. Like all the magic numbers, it's been there so long it's hard wired. Twelve months in a year. Twelve eggs in a carton. Twelve disciples for Jesus. Twelve doughnuts in a box. Whoever, whatever is causing this is surely aware of the significance of twelve even if only on a subconscious level."

"And what if you're wrong? What if it's more? A lot more? Hundreds? Thousands?"

Gelb cocked his hairless eyebrows, "Let's not get our hopes up, Mr. President."

"So tell me what we're gonna do. This thing's taking off and we don't have control. The War on Christianity. The New

Dark Ages. The War Between Good and Evil. Christianity on the Brink. Shit's gettin real."

"More like the War *Between* the Christians," said Gelb.

"The media, Hollywood liberals, just stirring the pot, Mr. President," said Herschfeld.

"Smoking the pot, Herschbo. Smoking the pot."

Gelb farted, louder and longer than he expected to, thinking that he could pull it off *en silencio*, as it were.

Herschfeld took several steps away.

"So what are we going to do about it?" the president asked again.

"Why do anything, Mr. President?" Herschfeld stood in the middle of the Oval Office, arms crossed in deliberation. "Let it play itself out. Buy some time. See what happens. Let them blame it on the liberals. God hates liberals. Don't get between God and his people. Talk big, do little. Hollywood liberals and pot smokers," said Herschfeld. "Why not?"

"Too general, Herschbo. Where's the bad guy? Red meat. Somebody we can insinuate without evidence. Who's been running his mouth?" asked the president.

Herschfeld was calculating, "Bill Maher has a new shtick, fits the profile, says religion is the next one to fall. Says, first they got pot. Then they got gay marriage. Could be him. Left wing. Got the money. Got a hardon for good, honest, hard-working Christians. Says they're ridiculous. Did a movie about them. Smug bastard. Blame it on him."

"Bill Maher?" asked Gelb, unaware of who they were talking about.

The president answered, "Liberal comedian. Not funny if you ask me but the PBS crowd likes him. Have to admit, he's always come across as a subversive wannabe to me."

"So what are we going to do?" asked Herschfeld.

The president thought for a second, "Throw him a sack of shit, Herschbo, why not?"

Herschfeld nodded in the affirmative.

"But that still doesn't address the problem, Mr. President, our core problem," said Herschfeld.

"And what's that?" asked the president

"The danger is, one of the Shopping Center Churches will luck up, reach critical mass and overwhelm the system. Osmond was a pussy boy. He'd already made his nut, wasn't-in-your-face power hungry. Wasn't his brand. But these new guys are vicious. It's all a video game to them. One of them gets loose, makes a run, who knows? Christian Dominionists control the Officer Corp already, have since Reagan. Pentagon is full of them."

"We need an end run, Mr. President," said Herschfeld.

The president nodded to the door, "Thank you, Mr. Gelb. Stay in touch."

Gelb left.

"So what else you got for me Herschbo?"

"Mississippi wants to secede," said Herschfeld, flipping through his notes.

"Tell Mississippi to kiss my ass."

"They say you let California go, why can't they?

"Nobody from California votes for us. Mississippi's solid Tea Klux Klan."

The president thought a minute, "Give 'em another oil refinery or a nuclear waste site, keep 'em happy."

"Understood, Mr. President."

Herschfeld walked to the door, stopped halfway, turned and said, "It's getting complicated, Mr. President."

"Indeed it is, Mr. Herschfeld. Indeed it is."

| The Sign

SHE HAD TO GO.

But first, she thought she should say something to the old man sitting in front of her.

On the other hand, it might be best not to get started. The last person she had spoken to was a belligerent commode and that hadn't ended well. Plus, she thought he should go first. It was only right. Good manners.

She looked at him.

He looked up at her, head poking from his coat, eyes barely visible beneath the brim of his cap.

She closed her eyes, held them shut, counted to ten and opened them again. He was still there. Must be real.

She made a point of gazing back and forth, focusing on nothing in the distance, as if he were not there.

He was making her nervous.

From across the plaza, more came, in ones and twos, a couple of winos who may or may not have been in a committed relationship, a few teenagers, parents with children. They gathered around the others already there, sitting cross-legged, mostly quiet, sometimes whispering among themselves.

The snow picked up, in gusts and swirls.

Suzze lifted her feet up onto the bench and drew the robe close around her, crossing her arms to hold it shut.

Her nose dripped down her lips.

She stared down at the old man. Talk to me old man, talk to me goddammit.

Nothing.

She still had to go.

There was a communal toilet across the plaza behind an ornamental apple tree which sat in a concrete planter, the unpicked fruit still clinging but wilting and rotting.

Should she go?

Maybe.

Maybe not.

Why not? If she did, maybe he would be gone when she got back.

She made her way through the gatherers, across the plaza and behind the concrete planter.

She squatted and strained holding onto the edge of the planter for balance.

Nothing.

She waited.

She tried again.

Still nothing.

She realized how much she missed Hopkins at times like this and thought about little Matthew, wondered how he was doing.

She sniffed and wiped her nose and strained some more and realized that it wasn't happening.

She stood to walk back to the bench but decided to skip out, time to move on.

She looked down a side street, then back at the people sitting on the ground, then down the side street, then back to the bench again.

No!

No!

She was here first.

Her bench.

Not theirs.

Hers.

Not his.

Hers.

Her bench.

She made her way through the crowd, or what was quickly becoming a crowd, head held high, shoulders back, and resumed her position, on her bench, them on the ground, snow blowing, noses running, her bench.

She sucked her nose and wiped it with the back of her hand.

She glared down at the old man, still determined that he would speak first.

Nothing.

She gazed again across the group gathered at her feet, as one by one others came and sat in ever expanding circles around her.

Okay, let's get this over with. No need to stand on her laurels. Come to think of it, any laurels she ever had were long gone.

She looked down at the old man. "Hey, how about this weather, huh?"

He looked up, "They're looking for a sign," he said.

A sign?

What kind of sign?

A sign of what?

She peered into her robe, not looking for anything in particular but not knowing what else to do.

She itched.

She reached her hand into her robe and between her legs and scratched. She took her hand away, realized the itch was still there and put her hand back between her legs and scratched some more.

A little girl whispered, "What's she doing mommy?"

Suzze took her hand out, only mildly embarrassed, and regained her composure.

A sign.

She looked from side to side and across the plaza, at the blowing garbage, the paper, the plastic cups and bags.

There. There it was.

She pointed and the stringy-haired woman with the oil in her pocket picked it up and passed it, hand to hand, person to person back towards the bench. The little girl who had whispered to her mother handed it to her, handle first.

Suzze examined the blade and wiped it across her robe.

Wüsthof.

She closed her eyes.

She sniffed.

She thought about Grandmamma Eunice and Grandpapa Dwight. Gone now. Good riddance. And Joel. And mother. Where are you, mother?

She closed her eyes and tilted her head back. The snowflakes sparkled against her skin and melted into cold drops that ran across her forehead and down her cheeks and over her lips. So clean, so clean, so clean, she felt them wash the past away. Please God, please, please don't ever make me leave this perfect place.

She opened her eyes.

She was surprised. They were still there. Still sitting. Still whispering.

She wiped her nose across her sleeve.

She raised her feet, crossed her legs, dropped the bathrobe from her shoulders to her waist and arched her back, leaning forward, bolt upright.

She cupped her left breast in her left hand, lifting it upward. With the knife in her right hand, she held the blade flat against her ribs and pushed the tip into the bottom of her breast, sliding the three-inch blade all the way in.

Clear, thick, silicone drained from the slit where the knife still rested.

When it stopped, she inched the end of the blade left to right opening the incision until she could reach in with her thumb and forefinger and pull out the plastic sack that was left inside. She let it fall onto the bench between her knees where it sat for a few seconds before creeping over the edge and plopping onto the ground like a dead jellyfish.

She switched hands and cut the implant from her right breast and let it drop onto the ground beside the other.

She bled, but not much, and it soon stopped.

The snow was settling in her hair and on her shoulders.

She wiped her nose.

She looked at them, still silent, expressionless.

She stood and pulled the robe around herself.

The old man stood with her.

They walked to the edge of the plaza and started down a side street.

One by one the gatherers rose and walked along behind them, keeping a respectful distance. As they did a piece of paper rose and blew among their feet, a piece missing from the magazine Suzze had cast into the wind earlier that day. It reported that a book, 'The Wars of The Parties of God: A

Current History' by Heifetz and Aslan, selling only in digital editions for 99¢ adjusted in all major foreign currency equivalents had topped the Amazon all-time bestseller list, having sold or otherwise distributed thirty-two million copies in dozens of languages. Religious War was now the dominant theme in popular culture. But then, she knew that already.

Suzze nudged the Old Man. "What's your name?" she asked as they rounded the corner.

- - -

Exactly thirty days after the distribution of the stuffed Baby Jesus dolls, now known colloquially as Squeezy Jeezy, they each, synchronously, began to recite scripture from both the old and the new testament imploring the children to kill their parents and other nefarious acts, most notably Matthew 10:21, "and the children shall rise up against their parents, and cause them to be put to death."

Representative Hogg of Mississippi labeled the perpetrators, whoever they might be, "Atheist Terrorists" engaged in holy warfare and demanded a military response. The Department of Homeland Security was called to investigate. The Sons of Jesus stood guard in the halls of nursery schools and day care centers, constantly vigilant, firearms at the ready.

The Reverend Bufe Swaringen, pastor of the Pentecostal Worldview Church, a converted shoe store off the Highway 52 bypass in Moncks Corner, South Carolina held a burning. He enjoined his meager congregation, along with a large contingent of locals eager for press exposure, to collect the dolls, which they did, often from the arms of crying children, until there were several pickup trucks full.

The image of thousands of Baby Jesuses burning on the pyre, though perhaps not exactly the message the Reverend hoped to convey, was immediately the impetus for a hundred conspiracy theories, most notably from Mike Huckabee, who was unsure of what it was but positive it was something.

Fundamentalist intellectuals disagreed over the origin of the demons, who sent them, and where they came from. But the one thing they agreed upon without dissent was that the Antichrist surely walked among them.

Episode 2

Captain Audaciousburger

Scenes

- - -

Despite cease and desist orders from attorneys representing the intellectual property of Camel in a Haystack LLC (aka Prosperity Cathedral), Sarah Gonzales first incorporated, then branded her enterprise SuzzePoops, Inc. ($150 online). She expanded her suzzewear.com product line to include x-large to xxx-large as well as children's sizes; then designed gold-seamed luxury "SuzzePoops" bathrobes for $249.99 which included a complimentary sample of her new line of Suzze-themed hair care products.

Telling her rags to riches (no-pun-intended-ha-ha) story in a two-hour cycle on Home Shopping Network generated 102,000 orders give or take. Allowing for a standard 25% return and other fees, she collected a one-day paycheck of over $400,000.00 which would stand as her personal best throughout her career.

She moved her family to a middle-class neighborhood in Orlando, rented a warehouse-shipping facility on a short-term lease and signed up for twenty hours a month on Net Jet.

| Detroit

"JACK? IS THAT SHORT FOR JOHN? A lot of times, Jack is short for John. So is it Jack, like, *just Jack,* or is it Jack, as in short for John?"

"Jack's good."

Suzze noticed that the Old Man waddled, bouncing back and forth as he walked. "How'd you get to be so bowlegged, Jack?"

He ignored her.

Suzze looked over her shoulder. The people who had been following them were no longer there.

"Okay Jack, so where are we?"

"It looks like Detroit."

"Never been to Detroit, Jack."

"Neither have I."

"Why are we in Detroit, Jack? And how did we get here?"

"I screwed up."

"I got that part, Jack. How?"

"Wrong turn."

They were on a bad street in a bad part of town, empty storefronts, broken glass and garbage. Black ice streaked the pavement.

"Now I know who you're trying to be. That detective guy who was on TV when I was a kid. He had that same raincoat and a ratty old hat. Why are you acting like him, Jack? Why don't you just be yourself? Everybody likes someone who is genuine, Jack. And I don't think you're being genuine with me. Does that make sense?"

"I understand."

"Stand up straight and quit mumbling."

"I will."

"You still didn't tell me how we got to Detroit, Jack."

"Negative energy, positive energy, I'll show you sometime," the Old Man mumbled, looking left and right, up and down the street. He heard something from behind. Soft. Feet maybe. On wet pavement. He stopped so that he could hear the footsteps above his own.

Suzze was ten steps ahead before she realized he was no longer by her side. She turned. The Old Man was fishing in his pockets. He pulled out what appeared to be the sash to her bathrobe and held it out.

He walked toward Suzze. "Here. Put this on."

"What's that Jack?"

The Old Man made a point of eyeing Suzze up and down through the gap in her robe, "Just put it on."

Suzze looked down at herself, her feet, her crotch, her breasts, still oozing, "Do we have a problem, Jack? Because it's a little early in our relationship to be having problems, know what I mean. I…"

"Just put it on. We're not in the garden anymore."

Suzze made a snoot, snatched the sash from his hand, wrapped it around her waist and adjusted the robe intentionally leaving a small but noticeable gap, refusing to hide her nakedness completely.

"I gotta go, Jack."

"Not now."

"Now, Jack."

"Can't it wait? I'd like to get out of here and that might take a while."

Suzze bounced up and down, looking back and forth for a spot that would give her a moment's privacy. Before the Old Man could say anything, she ducked into an alley and squatted behind a dumpster. The bottom was corroded through. Heat vapor rose off festering slime, the end product of rot that dripped onto the pavement and pooled under the dumpster before making its way down an open manhole and into the bowels of the earth.

It was obvious that she was not the first to have used the facility.

After getting herself situated, she started talking again, calling out from behind the dumpster loud enough to make sure the Old Man heard her, "I still don't understand how we got here, Jack. Energy? What does that mean? You mean like time travel? Did we just zap somewhere Jack? To another dimension of time and space? Are you a space traveler, Jack? Do you, like, do you travel through space and time?"

"I mean like getting lost."

"Oh please God, Jack, tell me you've got an iPhone or MapQuest or something."

"I'm working on it." The Old Man stayed on the opposite side of the dumpster, standing guard, facing the street, hiding in the shadows of a sodium streetlight that was buzzing from the far end of the alley.

"Are you a Catholic, Jack? Did you know that Catholics have a special holy water enema to exorcise the devil from your butthole? It's true. They do. I read it on the Internet. You can Google it if you don't believe me."

"I believe you."

The Old Man glanced from side to side, uneasy, no one in sight. Mostly old storefronts, abandoned cars, the pavement covered with a low, damp, stinking fog.

"Hey, Jack?"

He heard a crash and voices approaching from down the street.

"Shush. Be quite."

He peeked around the edge of the building.

She whispered, "Jack, I'm gonna need some TP or something."

"TP?"

"Paper, Jack. You know."

"Do you have to talk so much?"

"It helps to take my mind off it. It's easier for me if I don't have to think about what I'm doing."

"Gotcha."

"Catholics talk to God, Jack. You ever talk to God?"

"Every day."

"Oh yeah? What does he say?"

"Be nice."

"That's it?"

"What else do you need to know?"

"You're funny Jack."

"I used to talk to my commode."

"Did it talk back?"

"Yes, he did."

The Old Man shook his head and gazed skyward but there was no sky, no stars, just haze a hundred feet above his head.

"But we had a falling out."

The lid on the dumpster was warped open. The Old Man

reached in careful not to touch the fetid sides and pulled out a newspaper. As he lifted it, the outer sheets fell away and he was left with a relatively clean advertising insert.

He folded the paper back and forth along the seam, then ran his thumbnail down the fold for a sharp crease, then made a neat tear which left two smaller pages, one in his right hand, one in his left.

Whatever was down the street was getting closer. He peeked again. Nothing.

He held the pieces together. It was an ad for *The Road to Prosperity* at Joe Louis Arena. On one half was a headshot of big-toothed Joel, on the other half, big-haired Suzze, each beaming from ear to ear. The Old Man studied the paper, then looked up past the fog that obliterated the stars, smirked, shook his head in silent communication and mouthed the word 'cute.'

"I thought you said you'd never been here." He was speaking to Suzze.

"Where, Jack?"

"Here."

"Here where?"

"Here. Right here. Here, in Detroit."

"Don't get snotty, Jack. I thought you meant *here* behind this dumpster, *here* in this godforsaken shithole you made some zippy zappy wrong turn and brought me to. No, I've never been *here*, Jack. I've never been to Detroit. Joel and me, we were on a tour and this might have been on the schedule. I don't know, I didn't keep up with stuff like that. We had people for stuff like that. But when Joel blew up they canceled everything, so no, Jack, I've never been to Detroit and I hope to hell I never come back. Now quit bothering me. I need to concentrate."

"Waiting on you."

Whatever was down the street was getting closer.

"You know Jack…"

"Be quiet."

Suzze whispered, "You know Jack, I really loved him, I really did, in a way. I thought he was my ticket out, and he was, so maybe it was a good deal for both of us. We made a really good team. You got to give us that. But it just got to the point where I didn't want it anymore. I was starting to ask myself, Is that all there is? You know that Peggy Lee song, Is that all there is? And then it says, if that's all there is my friend then let's keep dancing, and then they bring out the booze and they have a ball? Well, I mean, I had the booze and I had the dancing and sometimes I was having a ball. Looking back on it now I see that I was but it's not what I want to do. Not now. Not anymore. Maybe it was what I wanted to do then. I mean, I was young and I had no idea what I wanted to do except get away from where I was. That's what I wanted to do, and Joel was the way out, but I knew I couldn't go on with it anymore and I was going to leave him, Jack. I never told anybody but I was going to leave him. When all this happened I'd already made up my mind. I was going to be Suzze. Just Suzze. Solo. Like Oprah is just Oprah. And I was thinking about it more and more and was ready to go, ready to make my move, and then his freaking head exploded right there in front of me and I'm thinking Christ Almighty did somebody just hand me my ticket out of town or was it a sign from God and I'm next?"

The Old Man held the paper by the edges in both hands, scrunching it and kneading it between his knuckles, breaking up the fibers of the newsprint until it was Charmin soft.

Suzze's whispers grew louder the more she talked. "And I'm scared to death Jack. Or I was. And I'm thinking, either way, it's time to get back to where I belong."

"That's sort of what I have in mind too. Keep it down," said the Old Man.

The sounds from down the street grew louder, closer. The Old Man peeked around the corner again. Three kids. Hoodies. Baggy pants. Expensive sneakers. They were coming up on the other side of the street, banging cars, breaking windows, having a good time. The Old Man froze, standing motionless as the kids walked past him, down the street and out of sight, making too much racket to notice him standing in the shadow of the alleyway.

"Uh, Jack, uh, I'm finished here and…"

The Old Man held the newspaper behind his back and took a couple of steps backwards to reach around the corner of the dumpster without turning around.

Suzze took the newly minted toilet paper from his hands, "Thanks, Jack, you're a lifesaver."

He stepped forward and peeked down the street again. Quiet. Nothing.

The Old Man stepped back to the front of the dumpster.

The kid was standing in front of him, tall, sickly, skinny, gums eroded, welts on his face. Over his shoulder, the old man saw the other two at the back entrance to the alley backlit from the streetlight. Smart. Pack behavior. Circle around. Surround the prey. Keep your distance. Send out a scout.

The kid grinned and nodded towards the back of the dumpster, a gleam in his eye. He held a tire iron in his right hand. He reached out his left hand and motioned for the old man to give it up.

The Old man looked down at the tire iron. Why do low tech? At the least he should have a Glock or a Sig. Maybe it was supposed to look like a mugging or an assault by homeless carnivores.

The Old Man nodded in resignation and fumbled deep in his left pocket. He looked up at the kid and shrugged. Nothing there. He reached deep into his right pocket and shrugged again.

The kid glanced back over his shoulder to summon the others. As he did, the Old Man grabbed the tire iron with his left hand, pulled the paring knife from his right pocket and jammed it squarely under the kid's breastbone. The kid looked down, dumbfounded. The Old Man stared up at him, maintaining eye contact, pinching his tongue between his teeth, concentrating, probing for just the right spot.

There.

The kid's eyes rolled back.

The Old Man smelled his last breath as it expelled with a gush, then his urine as it soaked his pants.

The kid's knees buckled dropping him even lower onto the blade.

His buddies stopped, turned, and ran.

The Old Man let go of the iron. It clanked to the pavement.

"What was that, Jack?"

The Old Man grabbed the kid by the front of his hoodie, "Vade in pace," he whispered as he rolled the kid backward, down onto his haunches. As he slipped to the pavement, as if in slow motion, the Old Man noticed a tattoo on his neck, a cross and the word 'Evolve'.

The kid bled out fast, his blood black under the orange sodium light mixing with the drippings from the dumpster.

The Old Man wiped the knife across the kid's pants and put it back in his pocket. He nudged the kid's limp body head first down the open manhole. The splash was louder than he expected. He looked up, then left and right. Nobody there.

He could hear Suzze's bare feet slapping against the wet pavement.

"Thanks, Jack."

The Old Man swiveled a quick right around the corner of the dumpster to head her off and point her out of the alley.

"Really. For everything. Thanks for listening. You're a good listener, Jack."

He wrapped his arm around hers, elbow to elbow, and led her out of the alley and down the street without looking back.

Part way down the block she stopped suddenly, which stopped the Old Man too and nudged him so they were standing face to face. "You know what I think, Jack? I think we need a plan."

"A plan?"

"Yeah, a plan. Highly effective people always have a plan."

The Old Man shrugged.

Suzze started walking again, still arm in arm, now with her head on the Old Man's shoulder. "Let's go someplace warm, Jack."

As they walked down the street, they looked like nothing so much as two people who had just shared an intimate moment.

"Jack?"

"Yes, Susan."

"You know that thing you did back there?"

"I…"

"It wasn't funny, Jack."

The Old Man paused for a beat, wondering what if anything

to say. "He thought it was."

"He? He who? Who you talking about, Jack?"

- - -

Police were dispatched to the Fort Worth home of Pastor Buddy Young when noise detection monitors reported hysterical screaming in a foreign tongue. Police arrived to find Giovanni Lombardi-Ferrara, Pastor Young's personal barista in the kitchen dressed only in his breakfast thong. According to Lombardi-Ferrara, speaking broken English between sobs, Young was in the kitchen sipping a Caffè Macchiato Chiaro with extra microfoam and hand-ground Korintje cinnamon hand-pulled by Lombardi-Ferrara himself from Young's Franke Evolution 1-Step Espresso Machine, when he puked ("vomitato") in his cup, reflexively snorted the swill back into his nose ("rigurgitare") and puked again prior to both eyes popping out, whereupon he fell to the floor, his chin striking the granite countertop on the way down, which peeled back his face and lifted off the top of his skull.

MSNBC had recently commented on the Reverend's purchase of the $19,500.00 coffee maker and his need for an experienced barista to operate it. "Hey, you want good coffee, you gotta pay the price," he said at the time.

Numerous blog posts accused Young of being ringleader of the Evangelist Mafia, though specifics are never offered, nor were other, supposed, members identified.

It was subsequently determined that Lombardi-Ferrara was a Catholic refuge. He has been remanded to ICE for repatriation.

| Captain Audaciousburger

PASTOR STEVE GAVE THANKS TO THE LORD. Now, with Joel gone, he was the biggest.

The biggest congregation.

The biggest bank account. (Accounts.)

The biggest house. (Houses.)

The biggest personal jet. (Jets.)

And truth be told, the biggest dick, though he left that to the imagination of the women – and truth be told again, the men – who wistfully gazed upon the bulge in his pants as he pranced and danced back and forth across the stage. He'd lead with his crotch (subtly, of course), give them a wink or a nod, then shoot them – *Pow!* – with his finger gun.

He never missed.

Still, it was a shame about Joel. Here one minute, gone the next. All he could figure was, Joel was boring the Lord. What better explanation? What bigger sin? His congregation was already scattered to the winds, preyed upon by every preacher with a past due Lear Jet payment. And Suzze? Suzze Woozy? Conveniently crazy. But, as he knew all too well, she always was. Not an issue. Out of the picture. But man was he going to miss those tits. Maybe he should give her a call.

Bottom line, he'd pick up half of Prosperity which would give him enough market share to slide into the number one spot. Truth be told, he'd have gotten there sooner than later.

His Evolution Church was growing at twice their rate, just a matter of time, but hey, favor is not fair, take God's blessings when he bestows them.

Enough about Joel, time to warm up.

Big room. Dressing room, rehearsal room, hardwood floors, mirrors floor to ceiling on one wall, projection screen floor to ceiling on the other.

Steve undressed.

The door buzzed and a nameless wardrobe assistant came in with a rack of clothes in tow.

He slipped on his True Religion Peg Leg Jeans (He loved the inside joke and they were only $188.00 in black, the only color he wore), stepped into his Vintage Nike High Dunk Ultimate Glory's ($449.95 online, cheap, real cheap for vintage Nikes, in paint crackle red, orange, or yellow, twelve pairs, give them time to air out between shows) and pulled on a black silk T-shirt (a Dolce and Gabbana knockoff, why pay $1,495.00 when his tailor in Hong Kong could crank them out a dozen at a time for only eight-hundred bucks?).

Vestments make the man.

He bounced up and down to settle his junk and snapped his pants. No belt. No socks. No underwear.

Julie (Was it Julie? Suzanne? Peggy? He could never remember.) entered to artfully mousse and muss his hair so that it looked as if he had just gotten out of bed, which, likely, he had.

He leaned in to the mirror.

He nodded.

He approved.

He pointed his finger toward the mirror and shot himself with his finger gun. *Ka-pow! In-de-struc-tible.*

Was he?

Yes, he was!

He adjusted the hood to his hoodie ($3.00 used from the Salvation Army, Steve was a man of the people), stretched the waistband until it was noticeably askew and then spun twice, heel and toe, eyes closed, opening them as he came out of his pirouette to see himself anew.

Instant rebirth. *Bang, bang, bang. There. He. Was.*

Was he slicker than owl shit? Yes, he was. *Swish, swish, swish. Pow. Pow. Pow. Au-da-cious!*

He mugged. He posed. He mimed.

He looked surprised.

He looked sincere.

He was caught off guard. *Who? Me?*

He was bold. *Yes! Me!*

He was passive.

He was aggressive.

He was penitent.

He was humble.

He pranced. He danced. He glanced.

He did a double-take. *I don't believe it.*

He chuckled.

He laughed.

He wept. (As only a real man can.)

He understood. (Lips pursed, eyes closed, pain real.)

He was ready.

Theater arts had served him well. He studied privately under the masters (YouTube videos), prancing from Mick, moonwalking from Michael, improv from Colbert.

And surprise – feigned or otherwise – from the great goddess of the known universe herself, Oprah Winfrey. Hel-lo-oh-oh! 'You don't become what you want, you become what you believe.' (Yes, she really said that.)

Indeed, Pastor Steve stood on the shoulders of giants and the view was spectacular.

Pastor Steve – dare we speak the words, "Saint Steve"? – had managed to do what all the other Pop-Up Churches had not, achieve critical mass and assemble a marketing machine to outgun the Prosperity Cathedrals, the once-prominent Lakewoods, the Willowcreeks, the Saddlebacks, the New Hopes. (Call them Old Hopes for they had No Hope, for Pastor Steve had them in his sights. Ka-Pow! Blow the smoke away.)

Unlike the other Name It and Claim It churches, Steve had developed and now operated off a modified Amway model. Like them, he still did direct debit, a percentage of your income, an investment in your future. Call it God's 401(k). (He and Pudge had been angel investors in eTithe.)

But Steve took it one significant step further.

Want to start your own church? Why bother when Pastor Steve can set you up with nothing down and no overhead?

Bring them in. Sign them up. Friends and Family for God. They get an instant prize. You get an instant bonus with lifetime residual income. Levels for Pre-School, Young Adult, and Warriors for Christ. (Over 40? Maybe you had a place. Over 50? Steve just wasn't interested. Over 60? That's over the hill.)

It was all Steve's idea. (Or Pudge's, depending on who you wanted to believe.) Theoretically, mathematically perhaps, the day might come when there would be no more converts to sign up, no more downstream income for the grunts who were out there beating the bushes like Saint Paul, converting the masses and collecting their reward. But by that time, he would have millions of Warriors for Christ and bigger fish to fry.

The mega-churches with their giant stadiums and unsustainable overhead would be but a memory, their income dying off with their aging populations.

Steve twirled from the mirror to face the latest video projected onto the opposite wall.

"And our enemies are all around us," firm and affirmative without shouting.

'Enemies.' The word had been focus-group tested multiple times on multiple platforms. Always testing high, it was repeated eleven to fourteen times during each sermon, concentrated in the last ten minutes of every twenty-minute segment.

"Let Jesus defeat your enemies and bestow upon you the rewards that you, his true followers, hunger for and deserve." Pastor Steve scanned the script which crawled across the bottom of the screen. Might need some work. It didn't flow.

The script itself was largely computer generated, outlined from topics that were currently trending on the Internet, then blended with words both poetic and archaic, a combination that sounded both profound and biblical.

During the sermon, eTithes were monitored in real time to see which keywords were most effective.

'Sin,' 'salvation,' and 'brotherhood' tested poorly and were rarely if ever used.

'Enemy' tested well.

'Reward' performed better, near the top.

But 'Receive' blew them off the charts. (It was the classic free lunch. Six-thousand, four-hundred and twenty-seven years since creation and everybody still wanted one.) And Pastor Steve delivered. No, his Lord and Savior, Jesus Christ delivered, if only you were Audacious enough to ask.

In Pastor Steve's world, Audaciousness was the determining factor. How much you might receive depended on that factor and that one factor alone. One needed supreme Audacitivity. And if your Audacious Audaciousness was not enough, then you should start eating Audaciousburgers. (The obtuse point being that you needed to commit your very being to being audacious.) (Christians love obtuse. With it, you can explain anything.) And if even that wasn't enough, the next step was to smother your Audaciousburger in Audaciousauce, which made them, (You guessed it) Audaciolicious.

It was logical.

It made perfect sense.

It was also the subject of Pastor Steve's first mega-best seller, 'Captain Audaciousburger'. The sequel, 'Audaciousauce for Your Audaciousburger', generated enough advance orders to make it an instant hit, driven by massive in-house purchases (they bought a hundred-thousand copies from themselves), which they then gave away Absolutely Free! to new members, thereby using their ad budget to create artificially high sales, which gave the impression of unprecedented demand, which in turn drove even more, legitimate, book sales, and so on, and on, and on, in a self-replicating cycle. (Now that's audacious!)

As Pastor Steve sashayed down the hall toward the stage (excuse me, pulpit), he silently acknowledged the nameless people in windowless offices behind secure doors.

At marketing subsidiary Audaciolicious Inc., a hundred bright-eyed and eager Geeks for God manned telephones and chat lines, responding to paid and natural search queries with offers for books, caps, t-shirts, family vacations and short-term loans, always with an up-sell, or a cross-sell, all for a modest increase in your monthly direct deposit. (Would you prefer a new iPad or three days in retreat to learn how to get ahead with Jesus directly from Pastor Steve?) They monitored and analyzed web hits in real time, optimized landing pages, and loaded blogs with computer generated content salted with inbound URLs to maximize SEO.

Access to Reputation Management housed only vetted media professionals bound by rigid non-disclosure agreements who diffused embarrassing questions and quelled malicious remarks, true or not.

Was Pastor Steve gay?

No. Pastor Steve was happily married to the love of his life and they enjoyed two wonderful children.

Had Pastor Steve ever done drugs?

Yes. But only once and he sought and received forgiveness and you can too.

How much does Pastor Steve make?

Pastor Steve's compensation is determined by an advisory board. (At which point, the inquiring party was automatically switched to a montage of videos praising Evolution's multitude of good deeds.)

eTithes was where the money was created, the cash cow, the

golden calf. Steve and Pudge had been angel investors and now owned 80% of the operation, undisclosed of course, with multiple levels of filters provided by multiple corporate entities scattered throughout the Caribbean. Not only did Pudge and Steve reach into the bank accounts of their own Evolution Church members, they franchised the service to hundreds of other religious and charitable organizations (their ownership unbeknownst to their competitors, of course) which enabled them not only to collect a fee for service but to data mine every contributor to every other organization. It was, perhaps, an unfair advantage.

Corporate sponsorships were managed through a small but very specialized law firm in Washington, DC. Certainly, a majority of congresspersons were eager to avail themselves to the insights that only Pastor Steve (along with his best friend, Jesus Christ) possessed.

When, rarely, Pastor Steve had a moment of self-doubt, as all good Christians do, he found solace and comfort in one thing he knew for sure – that it was his faith, his absolute and unquestioning faith in his Lord and Savior Jesus Christ that made it all possible. For Steven knew one thing to a cosmic certainty. No amount of money, or technology, or market research alone could achieve all this by itself. There was one critical ingredient that those who criticized him – try as they may through their rational reasoning – simply could not understand, and had not been able to understand since the time of the Greeks: It's personal. God has a million faces. That is His nature. We each get the God we deserve.

And nobody believed that more – more firmly, more purely,

more passionately, more gloriously, more completely, more devoutly – than did Pastor Steven Hadad.

He was, simply put, the real deal.

Ka-Pow!

| Give Me The Boy

LITTLE STEVIE WAS HIGH STRUNG.

Dressed in his birthday garb, a cowboy outfit from Walmart, complete with boots, chaps, a white hat and a pair of six-shooters, his mother was trying to get him to blow out all four candles while she fumbled with the camera.

Instead, he ran to the coffee table and knocked the knickknacks to the floor. Then to an end table where one sweep of his arm sent ashtrays flying, and then back to the first table where he'd mess up what he had already messed up and mess it up some more, hopping and stomping and jitterbugging back and forth and back and forth, pausing to spin and dance and sometimes wet his pants in his own little temper tantrum for the Lord.

His image bounced and flickered in the frame as his mother chased him with the camera in awe of his every move. "Stevie, you a bad boy." Little Stevie laughed out loud as he eliminated his birthday cake, candles flaring, sugar candy flowers and happy birthday letters cast asunder.

"You a natural born dancer, a prancer, and a romancer par excellence. You should go to New York City and dance on the broad way," she teased him in her Cajun accent. And when she realized what she had said, *dancin' on the broad way*, she grabbed him up in her arms and hugged him tight and said to the ceiling, "Oh Lord, please, please, please, please, please don't let my Little Stevie be one of them."

Little Stevie squirmed his way out of her arms and was at it again, running into the bedroom and grabbing the bible on his mother's bedside table, shredding the pages and casting them to a metaphorical wind, the pieces falling around him like confetti. He tossed over another table, broke another lamp and stomped the torn pages under his feet.

(Two decades later this heretofore unknown and forgotten video of a tender family moment was to somehow be found, digitized and posted on YouTube to the delight a multitude of followers who reveled at the sight of their very own Messiah in all his youthful glory.)

Sensing a star in the rough, Stevie's mama pumped enough Ritalin in her little prophet to calm him down and choreograph his every move and then took his little skit, first to backwoods churches as entertainment for revivals, and later to split the pot at fund-raising events.

It was wholesome entertainment, fun for the whole family. The rec room at the church was set up with tables and lamps and knickknacks donated by the women's auxiliary or scavenged from second-hand shops. Blasphemous versions of the bible, in other words, anything other than the King James, were collected for the shredding. Chicken was fried. Sweet tea was poured. The collection plate was passed. Sometime between the end of the potato salad and the beginning of the banana pudding, Little Stevie would make his appearance running amongst the tables, trashing the false idols and second-hand figurines, all the while cursing the devil and *Pow! Pow! Pow!* shooting him dead, his six-guns blasting way.

Where's the debel? Show me the debel!, he would cry out while standing amidst the rubble.

And first one, and then another, and then another penitent in search of salvation would creep and crawl forward in pain and in anguish proclaiming that the devil indeed inhabited their being, that the devil alone was responsible for their transgressions, and yes please, *yes hallelujah*, rid me of this devil inside. And as they approached the stage the Blessed Little Stevie would shoot them with his six guns, *Ka-pow! Ka-pow! Ka-pow!* admonishing the debel, threatening the debel, killing the debel inside, *Pow! Pow! Pow! His Will Be Done*, as the sinners and supplicants fell dead at his feet.

Little Stevie would strut and posture and examine the carnage that lay before him, men and women, boys and girls, writhing in agony as the devil refused to free their souls.

After pausing for a standard three-count, (count now, his mother had taught him, one, pause, two, pause, three, take a deep breath and…) he'd take careful aim and shoot, point and shoot, applying the coup de grace to each and every one, *Pow!* as he cried out, Out you debels! *Pow!* Out you filthy Satan! *Pow! Pow! Pow!* Then, after taking time to survey the havoc, he would slowly raise his arms, six-shooters pointing to Heaven for God Almighty to smile upon, and in a voice barely above a whisper, then growing in volume with each admonition, he cast new life into those who lay before him, certainly dead of spirit if not of body. Arise heathens! Arise you adulterers! Arise you fornicators! Arise you pitiful creatures, weak of flesh and void of spirit!

And magically, together, they would rise, as if young sprouts washed clean by the spring rain, the once filthy heathens and adulterers and fornicators rose and reclaimed their place in the here and now, a new being, a new tomorrow, having just been resurrected both of the flesh and of the spirit, now in full bloom, twirling and swirling, dancing their own little jig upon the scraps of blasphemy, themselves now stomping those defeated ceramic idols into the concrete floor.

And thus it came to be that Little Stevie's fame spread far and wide: *I died. I died right there and then I tell you, couldn't see a thing, couldn't hear nothing neither, and the devil had me. He had hold of my heart. He corrupted my soul. And Little Stevie shot me. He killed the devil and gave me life. And I was reborn and Satan was gone and here I am. Blessed Stevie he saved me!*

That's the story they told, each one having heard it from the other and each one hearing it again and again as the former walking dead spread their testimony for all who would listen, for all those seeking truth. Could there be any doubt? they asked in the pews as the collection plate circulated.

And they questioned each other and they questioned themselves, wondering what their own impending death would be like, wondering if they, like those who died before them, would also see the devil, face to face, eyeball to eyeball, and wondering if they too would be resurrected, the devil inside having been blown to smithereens at the hands of the Blessed Little Stevie and his miraculous six guns.

They approached the question logically and rationally until their belief was firm and proved to them their salvation was at hand. And if that wasn't enough, they reminded each other that, in the end, after all, he was God's very own Little Cowboy. What was there to doubt?

After a few years of playing to packed houses, and filling their pews with flocks in need of a good blowing away, yet having earned only a handful of tens and twenties to show for all their effort, the Devil himself called upon the Blessed Little Steve.

There was, at that time, a small, failing ad agency in Biloxi, Mississippi by the name of Jay, Walter & Herschfeld, themselves destitute and all but unemployed, having a single small, failing client, a fast food joint named Audaciousburger, the hook being that every two-pound patty of questionable origin was served with Audaciousfries and a triple pack of their secret Audaciousauce, an Audacious dining experience verging on the divine.

It wasn't working, and all the dancing burgers and catchy headlines and focus groups of three-hundred- pound teenagers couldn't figure out what was wrong. Until…

Until Herschfeld, the creative head of the three-man shop had a drug-induced epiphany while sleeping one off in the back seat of his ten-year-old American Motors Matador. His Muse, Cassandra, reminding him that his demographic was 92% Jesus freak, largely illiterate and altogether gullible, whispered in his ear, *Give them a serving of the Holy Spirit with those burgers and fries*, she said to him.

Inspiration flew into action. A cattle call for "Cute Kid to Play Christ" was broadcast to talent agencies throughout the South. Little Stevie won the day, his mama signing the contract as his guardian-slash-manager, a contract that guaranteed Mother and Child not only a high degree of creative control but a piece of the action in lieu of salary, which unbeknownst to them at the time, neither Jay nor Walter nor Herschfeld nor Audaciousburger had the ready cash to pay.

From Day One/Spot One, it was a hit, with Little Stevie knocking over Hardee's Six Dollar Southwest Patty Melt Thickburgers, Carl's Low Carb Turkeyburgers, and whacking Jumbo Jack's before macerating the Great Satan itself, a Big Mac combo with fries and a Coke. He danced among the rubble, stomping puny little cartons of regular fries and sending 32 oz. Cokes flying before pouncing on the pitiful half-pound patties.

After pausing for his well-rehearsed three-count, he'd take a bite out of a burger too big for him to hold, look skyward and swoon, *au-dacious* as if it had been crafted in Heaven's own kitchen.

Once again Little Stevie hit his target of uneducated, overweight bible-thumpers by serving up four-thousand calories of their two favorite food groups, sugar and grease.

It made Little Stevie and his mama a boatload of money as the chain expanded to over a hundred outlets. Sunday, after church, the drive-through was packed. Inside, Contemporary Christian music filled them with the spirit of the Lord. Little Stevie, now Pastor Steve, a self-appointed preacher in name only (but who's to check his credentials?) would make guest appearances, personally blessing each and every combo meal as he passed out free packs of Audaciousauce to lather over those Audaciousfries. For a while, God was in his Heaven (having an Audaciousburger, of course) and all was right with the world.

Then came the plagues.

One by one, the outlets suffered outbreaks of Salmonella, then E. Coli, and then Botulism. As stores closed, rumors grew. There was talk of satanic rituals. A renegade minister, seeking to upstage Pastor Steve by himself exorcising the demons from the Audacious Chattanooga Outlet, slipped on a six-pack of Audaciousauce, fell and broke his back in three places, God's revenge to be sure.

What would come next, Ebola?

Well, actually, yes.

Unsubstantiated rumors, spread by yet another jealous lay-preacher with his sights set on his own fast-food empire did in the remaining stores. Although he nor anyone else was ever able to produce the first microbe that resembled an Ebola virus, he *preached* it to be true, science be damned, and so the faithful followed. A man of God does not deceive. A man of God does not lie.

The stores dropped like flies. The penitents packed into their pick-ups and paraded back to Popeye's.

Steven Hadad, as it turned out, though rich beyond his wildest dreams, was only rich on paper. And now his paper was worthless. And so was he.

Ka-poof!

Pastor Steve had shot his wad.

| Genesis

"IT'S A PONZI SCHEME, PUDGE, AND IT WON'T FLY."

Williford sat across the desk from the professor assigned to judge him as he flipped through the pages, decorating them with question marks, exclamation points, vague observations and snide comments.

So much for Williford's dream. He gouged at the back of his hand, at a scab that never healed, as he watched his pride and joy, his business plan to reinvent the church, being trashed by a third-rate academic.

Sheindlin, the professor, closed the folder, scratched an F across the top, marked that out and replaced it with a D, then a D+, finally settling on a C, stopping with the highest grade he could in good conscience bestow.

After watching Williford schlep through four years as a Financial Ministries major, his advisor, Sheindlin had come to the realization that Williford was one step below hopeless, but he couldn't flunk him out. Nobody flunks out of BJU – unless they're caught fornicating.

"It's trash. It's garbage. But nobody fails here, Mr. Ransom. Everybody passes. But I'd consider a new career if I were you. It won't fly. It's a Ponzi scheme. No reputable church would operate this way."

Williford considered countering his conclusion by questioning the existence of reputable churches but thought

CONNIE WELLBORNE & CHERRY SANTANA

the better of it.

"Amway's a Ponzi scheme and it flies quite well, doesn't it?" Williford knew he was skating on thin ice, questioning this imbecile who lorded dominion over him.

Sheindlin, the school's token Hebrew, fearful of losing his only hope for employment in the current economy, was fifty-eight years old, a man who had suffered four layoffs since he was forty, a man with no pride left, a man who gladly taught only what God wanted to be taught, the way God wanted it taught. After all, this was the college that sent a young Billy Graham on his way to pollute the world. It was a job. It was a job. It was a job.

"And evolution?" he asked. "Evolution! Forget it. You can't say evolution and God in the same sentence. Not if you ever expect to get a job. Plus, the word is banned here at BJU – don't worry, I'm not going to turn you in."

Bob Jones University. Harvard of the Holy Rollers.

He hated the place.

He hated the professors. (Them that can, do. Them that can't, teach.)

He hated his classmates.

He hated the routine.

He hated the ridiculous curriculum and the childish bible stories passed off as fact.

He hated his mother for condemning him to this hell on earth. She sent him, she said, so that he might dwell for four years – four long, miserable years that to him seemed like four-thousand – so that he might dwell in the house of the Lord who would surely cure him of his myriad afflictions. On the other hand, it was better than living with her.

He hated his life.

But most of all, he hated being called Pudge.

Williford 'Pudge' Ransom was, well, pudgy. Not fat. Flaccid. Short. Pale. Low muscle tone.

As a teenager, a granuloma had formed on his penis, the result of his endless stroking in search of sexual satisfaction which never came. His incomplete sexual development was a blessing to his mother, who assured God that her son, like His own, would also be pure of spirit and chaste of flesh.

Unable to satisfy his penis, and after his mother's constant admonishment to quit picking at himself through his pants, he switched, first to his nose, retrieving buggers with enough fury to deviate his septum, then to a mole on the side of his neck, one he couldn't see but could certainly feel, always there, an imperfection he could not tolerate, as bit by bit he clawed it away until it exposed his carotid artery.

Whenever he was tense or stressed or wanted to emotionally visit another place, he peeled away bits of his body, ingesting them afterward so as not to lose his essence.

It brought him peace.

Sheindlin was a fool. A man with no vision. It was a good plan. What did the Jew know? You'd think he'd know how to run a business. For what is a church, if not a business?

Pudge had a vision.

A church Evolved.

A church that showed you how to live your life above mere Christians.

A church that entered your life and claimed your soul.

A church that never let go.

He had done his homework.

He read the bible, watched the videos, reviewed the blogs.

He found inspiration in the life of Shau'l of Tarsus and his magnificent metamorphosis into Saint Paul.

He conducted a comparative analysis of all the Abrahamic religions, then pitted them against Buddhism, and Hinduism, noting what each had to offer, their relative merits and liabilities. And when he was finished, he came to the same conclusion that Saint Paul had two-thousand years earlier, he could make more money as a Christian.

Like Saint Paul before him, he needed a man, a man pure of heart, both naive and ambitious.

Did such a man exist?

Could such a man be found?

And if found, would he make the sacrifice?

All unanswered questions.

All creation was waiting to unfold, his creation, his vision, his dream, adoring him, blessing him, joining with him, two as one.

As he lay on the floor, waiting for the sleep that rarely came, his probing finger traveling from his penis to his mouth and back again, the question repeating itself in a never ending cycle for a thousand years that, to Pudge, was but a single day – Oh my beloved, where art thou?

| The Bizzle

PUDGE WAS LURKING IN THE SHADOWS.

It was approaching midnight, maybe later, but Pudge was biding his time, waiting days, weeks, a hundred years to be sure his entry into this forbidden world would go undetected.

He was not good at keeping time and place in sequential order. Which came when and what came where? It mattered not. He was of a time before time. The high priests knew not. When they came to him in their white robes and rubber gloves, their faces masked to hide their shame, they told him that what was for him a thousand years was, for them, only a day. Pudge forgave their ignorance of the natural world, confident and satisfied with the knowledge that soon unspeakable travesties would fall upon them.

And was it not for him to make his light known to the world, as his Church of Evolution would surely do?

He had the plan.

All he needed was an earthly corpus within which he could breathe the gift of outrageous success, a beautiful man worth making immortal.

And he knew that perfect clay was down there, somewhere.

He watched as a dozen students, alone and in couples, inched their way from the darkness, away from the lights, along the perimeter of the brick building, finally ducking into a bank of overgrown and untended shrubs before falling out of sight, into the earth, giggling as they disappeared.

If his powers of perception were as he supposed them to be, he would have been able to follow them, in his mind, as they wrapped their fingers around a steel door, the lock picked, someone's sneaker preventing it from snapping shut.

He would have walked along beside them as they stepped onto a steel landing, and then down a flight of open stairs onto yet another landing and down another flight of stairs. He would have inched his way behind ancient sewer pipes and underneath electrical conduit, the walls damp, the air musty, until he arrived at a place where neither he nor these youthful Bacchanals were meant to be. Or were they?

But he was still here, alone, in the darkness.

He waited another hundred years.

It was approaching midnight, perhaps later.

Tomorrow was the final day of BJU Presents Pastors of the Future, a biennial celebration of the best and the brightest that America had to offer.

He had checked them out, each and every one as they paraded around campus, chatting, pressing the flesh, blessing the students, sharing their favorite bible passages, explaining how they and their New and Improved brand of Christianity would surely change the world, making it ready once and for all for Christ their Lord, who they knew was eager to return as soon as they, personally, could establish their ministry and make Earth ready for him again. Pudge had followed them, listening to them, evaluating them, sniffing them, losers all, except for one, one who glowed with a divine light that Pudge had never beheld and he was blinded by it.

As he waited, working up the courage to confront his destiny, he nibbled at an ulcer on the back of his hand, small bites, soft scabs, fresh blood.

And his essence gave him strength.

And so he made his move.

He eased through the bushes to the steel door at the bottom of the half-flight of stairs. He opened the door just enough to step inside, unaware that his flat-footed gait had dragged away the sneaker propping the door open. The door slammed with a clunk that echoed down to the depths and back again.

He froze, then gouged a scab and rolled it between his teeth.

He heard voices, muffled, and then the voice magnificent, the object of his affection.

He proceeded slowly, step by step. The air was humid and hot and musty. With each step, the voices grew louder, muffled still but pleading, moaning, yearning.

There were pipes, water pipes and sewer pipes and ventilation pipes and dangling wires.

He heard a shriek and froze again, a female voice, perhaps in distress, pleading for more but begging for less.

He reached the final landing and stepped off, concealing himself, peering from behind a bank of metal cabinets.

He gouged at his septum, quieting his nerves.

He followed the mumblings and the giggles and the soft conversations coming from the dark corners and the anterooms and saw couples, students, two by two, four by four, some clothed, some shameful in their nakedness, some satisfying themselves, some satisfying each other, some watching, male with male, female with female, each with the other as if they were a single being conjoined in their filth.

And in the middle, glowing from the light of an eternal flame, an all but forgotten furnace fueled by gas from the bowels of the earth, sat Steve, Steven, Pastor Steve, a man of many names, a man of wondrous talents, a man of infinite beauty, sitting upon an old commode, another piece of detritus that had somehow made its way to the depths, like these lost souls, abandoned.

And those not copulating sat as his feet as he mugged and mimed, cajoling them, teasing them, seducing them before shooting each of them with his finger gun, shooting them dead, only to see them rise up again full of glee, laughing and pleading and asking for more.

After his crash, Steven Hadad had gone through several rounds of reinventing himself, most involving the copious consumption of drugs, only to end up peddling used cars, until he decided to go back to his roots, back to what he knew best, exchanging salvation for cash. It was a journey that had brought him here, here to the basement of Bob Jones University. He was here to build his base, to spread his gospel, to slay some bizzle and see if he could win a preaching contest.

Pudge remained still, silent, breathless, observing, confirming to himself that what he believed to be true was indeed true, that Steven Hadad possessed powers that mortal men do not.

The power to charm.

The power to enthrall.

The power to captivate.

The power to possess.

And just as it was adjudicated at the Council of Nicaea in A.D. 325, when the Christos, God the Son, was made one with God the Father, he, too, must meld with such a man, not only in spirit but also in flesh, no longer mortal men be they, but a single being, Man Become God.

As Pudge contemplated what lay before him, envisioning the

wondrous future that lay ahead, he plucked a dollop of coagulated blood from his septum and returned it once again to his body.

He wanted Steve alone, to himself.

How, he wondered, as he swallowed, savoring his essence, could he realize this destiny?

How, he wondered, could he separate Steven the Christos from the bleached blond bizzle currently stroking his turgid member...

- - -

Two weeks after a local option allowed prayer in the public schools in Lawrenceville, Kansas, ten-year-old Jessica Williams, known as a precocious child, pulled a vintage Mac-10 from her backpack and unloaded it into her teacher while all eyes were closed for daily devotionals, whereupon Williams walked outside, dropped the gun, raised her hands in defiance and proclaimed, "Nobody tells me to pray." She was shot nine times by school security officers and pronounced dead at the scene.

In a prepared statement, District 45 Representative Melanie Meigs (R), who spearheaded the prayer initiative said, "Gun control is not the problem. Jesus control is. Without the moral and ethical guidance that only Christ provides, atheistic behavior such as this can only be expected to increase. Losing young Jessica is a tragedy, but as long as America continues to turn its back on Jesus, as long as children are reared in households that know not the glory and power of our Lord, these incidents, this conflict, will continue."

Her constituency voiced its overwhelming support.

| Shroom, Shroom

"YOU'RE KIDDING ME, RIGHT JACK?"

The Old Man didn't answer.

"I said warm, Jack, let's go someplace warm." Suzze was walking in lockstep directly behind the Old Man.

"This is warm."

"And sunny. I wanted sunny," said Suzze.

The Old Man raised his arms in resignation, "This is sunny."

"This is the goddamned desert, Jack. It is not warm. It is hot. It is not sunny, it's…it's…it's not Aruba, Jack. Or Cancún. Or the Bahamas, Jack. It's the goddamned desert."

"It's sunny and warm," said the Old Man, stopping in the middle of the road.

A rusted Sinclair sign with a faded green dinosaur squeaked as it blew back and forth in front of a long-deserted service station.

The Old Man did a slow turn, hands to the sky, "I like it here."

"I don't, Jack. I don't like it here. I've seen this Jack, like, a thousand times. I get it. Lost in the wilderness. It's a cliché, Jack. You're a cliché, Jack. A cliché. Get over it. Whatever it is, get over it. Let's move on."

In the distance, a brown cloud settled on the ground.

Suzze looked around, still not liking what she saw, "How long we gonna be here, Jack?"

The Old Man examined the sky from horizon to horizon, "Hard to say. A couple of weeks, a month maybe."

"Ain't gonna happen, Jack. No way."

Frustrated, the Old Man grabbed Suzze by the shoulders, shaking her like a naughty child, "Just tell me, Susan. What do you want? Where do you want to go? What do you want to do? Who do you want to be, if not you?"

"I told you already, Jack. I want out. Out. Not out of my mind. Just out. I said I want to be nowhere, Jack, not in the middle of nowhere. It's a nuance thing, Jack. I was happy, Jack, on my little bench, in my little world, reading my little magazine, watching the little snowflakes fall. This isn't working out, Jack. I want to go home. Zap me back to where I came from."

Suzze shrugged her arms to loosen the Old Man's grip.

"How about you, Jack? How about you? What do you want? You haven't exactly shared with me if you know what I mean."

"I am but a voice crying in the wilderness."

"Oh, good grief. What does that mean? You're being ambiguous, Jack. I don't like ambiguous. You got a plan, tell me about it."

"Following the path."

"Jesus, Jack. It's derivative. Derivative, derivative, derivative. Cliché, cliché, cliché. Get over it."

Heat waves rose off the two-lane blacktop that stretched from horizon to horizon without a car in sight.

"Where's the buzzard, Jack? Don't you ever watch The Twilight Zone? There's supposed to be a buzzard circling overhead."

The Old Man was in pain. If anything, her drawl was even more intolerable when she whined. Did she ever not whine?

Suzze licked the sand off her lips and dry spit it towards the Old Man. She looked around surveying the immediate area, "I got to go, Jack."

"You're kidding me."

"I can't help it, Jack. Get used to it. It's me. It's who I am. It's what I do. You knew I was a snake before you picked me up. Right, Jack? That's what Joel used to say whenever he screwed up, 'You knew I was a snake before you picked me up.' Tell you the truth, Jack, he had a point."

The Old Man closed his eyes and begged silently.

Suzze shuffled around the side of the cinder block building, past dry-rotted tires, engines, mufflers, junk car parts and broken Coke bottles to the back of the service station. The door to the single toilet was caved in on its hinges. An Intimate Items machine hung crooked on the wall, cracked open, the change long gone. Dried out condoms and French ticklers in and out of their packs were strewn across the cement floor. The commode was dry as a bone.

Suzze decided to make the best of it, lifted her robe and half-squatted over the bowl, careful not to touch anything.

The Old Man stood silent outside the open doorway gazing towards the mountains, miles away.

A mangy dog walked up, sniffed them both, then licked at Suzze's feet. He stood there, head bowed, posturing for attention. Suzze tried to kick at him with one foot and maintain her balance with the other.

The dog arched his back, heaved several times and retched up a puddle of yellow bile, then gave every appearance of smiling at the Old Man before lapping it up again, with vigor.

He turned to Suzze, wagged his tail and lowered his head in supplication again expecting a pat and maybe a 'good boy.'

When he got neither food nor attention he cocked his leg toward the doorframe sending a stream of urine down the wall, across the floor, and between Suzze's feet, then trotted off, tail wagging.

The Old Man walked out into the desert leaving Suzze to her business.

She called after him, half yelling, "You asked me who I want to be, Jack. You know what? I like me, Jack. Tell you the truth, I like me. But if you mean who would I like to be if I wasn't actually me, then I've thought about it and I know who it is."

Whether he heard her or not, the Old Man didn't respond.

She called out louder, "I'll tell you who, Jack. Danica Patrick. That's who. The race car driver, Jack. That's who."

The Old Man walked a hundred steps more, then stopped, eyes to the ground. A storm rose behind the mountains. Lightning flashed, the thunder too far away to be heard.

A grasshopper lit on Suzze's shoulder. She brushed it away.

"She's a goddess, Jack. The woman's a goddess."

The Old Man took off his hat and coat and stood there naked as a jaybird, arms outstretched, looking up, facing the sun, his legs so bowed she could see daylight between them, his hairy ass hiding his private parts.

She glanced down to her feet and scrunched her toes, "Don't look up. Trust me, you don't want to see this."

Suzze called out again, "She can shift my gears."

The Old Man bowed his head.

Louder still, "Rev my motor."

The Old Man leaned over, flipped over a rock, picked up something, took a bite out of it.

Suzze cupped her hands like a megaphone, "Pump my clutch."

He stood up suddenly, snatched something from the air and put it in his mouth. Then another, munching on whatever it was as fast as he could pluck them from the sky.

When he had his fill he dropped to his knees, flipped over more rocks and scratched at the dirt, collecting the Earth's bounty.

"Slide into my pit."

The Old Man put his coat back on, dropped whatever he had into his pockets, dusted off his cap and turned and walked back towards Suzze.

"Okay, okay, I got it. You like Danica."

"Tell you the truth, Jack, I never did a girl before."

He was back, looking down at Suzze who was still half squatted over the seatless commode.

"At least not by myself."

"Are we about through?" The Old Man was growing tired of the chatter.

Suzze looked up, "Did you?"

He didn't answer.

"Susan, have you ever considered that your, uh, difficulties might not be all physical, that they might be tied to, perhaps, control issues?"

"You think if I go to Oz he can tell me what's wrong?"

"There are no wizards, Susan."

"Dr. Oz, Jack. Doctor. He's the one on TV. He's a poop whisperer. He had this movie star on and she walked out on stage carrying a whole plate full of stuff, her stuff which she had done backstage, all piled up. And Dr. Oz took a pair of chopsticks out of his pocket and he poked around in all those poopy pieces until he had them all separated. And then he stuck out his tongue and blew this white powder all over it and held it up and Lo and Behold all those pieces spelled words, and those words told her fortune. The man works miracles, Jack."

"There are no fortune tellers, Susan. The man augurs intestines. Hang a dead monkey around his neck and stick a bone in his nose, he's a witch doctor."

"Say what you will Jack, but I'm telling you, the man's a genius with a turd."

Suzze stood up and shook her butt letting her robe drop back into place, "Let's go, Jack. I can't do it here. I'd rather squat on a cactus."

The Old Man seized the moment and rounded the corner with Suzze two steps behind, still talking, "Let me ask you something, Jack. Are we lost? Again? Was this another wrong turn?"

"All who wander are not lost," said the Old Man.

"Cliché, cliché, cliché, Jack."

The Old Man stopped at the front of the service station, unsure of what to do next.

"Susan, let's talk for a minute."

He sat on one of the concrete islands, wires and pipes poking out of the holes where the gas pumps had been. He patted the cement, motioning for Suzze to sit beside him.

Suzze sat down, arms crossed, lips pursed, looking in the opposite direction.

"Since you brought it up, let's talk about the future. Your future."

He rested his hand on her knee.

"Have you given any thought to what's next?"

She jerked her knee away.

"Your future, Susan. Let's talk about that. What's

meaningful to you? What makes you happy? Where's your life headed? What are your goals?"

Suzze jumped up.

"Jesus H. Christ, Jack. What are you doing now, selling Amway?"

"I just thought…"

"Goals? Jack, goals are what got me in trouble in the first place. I don't have goals. I don't want goals. I'm going full blown Zen, Jack, like Gandhi."

"Gandhi was Hindu."

"Hindu Zendu Jack, it's all the same. No goals. No motivations. No thoughts. No worries. Empty, Jack. Nothing clogging my brain. And you know what, Jack? It feels great. It feels just freaking great, thank you very much, and I'm ready to go home now."

"Home?"

"I don't want to hear it, Jack. Home. I told you already, zap me back to where I came from."

"It doesn't work that way, Susan."

The Old Man stood.

"But follow me. I'll take you where you need to go."

They were back on the two-lane.

The Old Man picked up the pace.

Suzze fell in beside him.

The Old Man reached into his pocket and popped something into his mouth.

"I'm hungry, Jack."

He reached into his pocket again and pulled out a small dark lump, broke it in half and gave it to her.

"Damn Jack, where'd you get this?" She sniffed it, scrunching her nose at its musty fungal smell, then took a bite.

"Will it give me a buzz?"

The Old Man continued walking, tracking the center line, eyes on the vanishing point, *straight is the path.*

Thunder crashed as the storm grew closer. The wind picked up, slinging the sign back and forth faster and faster, the rusted hinges squealing like a siren. A cloud of brown locusts landed in front of them.

Suzze looked back at the service station and then over to the Old Man.

"Jack?"

"Yes, Susan."

"You can stop with the sign already. I get it. Cut the shit. Let's move on."

The sky cleared, the wind stilled and the sign stopped squeaking.

"For God's sake, Jack, can't we at least find a Motel 6 or something?"

The Old Man quickened his pace, as fast as his short, bowed legs would carry him, *straight is the path, straight is the path.*

|Friends

An hour later, the middle of the road, three miles out of town:
"SARA PALIN."

"You can't be serious."

"What's wrong with Sara Palin, Jack?"

"You're kidding me, right?"

"I kinda liked her Jack."

"Please, let's talk about something else."

"I like Danica Patrick better but I could go for Sara Palin. She kinda reminds me of my mom."

"Let's not go there."

"Okay, what do you want to talk about out here in the middle of goddamned nowhere? Speak to me Jack. Say something profound."

"You cannot travel the path until you have become the path." The Old Man was talking at her, not to her.

"Oh Jesus, Jack. I am the path. If I weren't the path, you wouldn't be dragging my ass down this road, know what I mean? I don't mind being the path, Jack. I mind you walkin' on me, Jack."

"Okay, how about 'What we think, we become.' Know who said that?" The Old Man was staring straight ahead huffing with every step.

"Oprah," said Suzze.

"Buddha," said the Old Man.

"Oprah, Jack. Oprah. It's like her signature saying. Where have you been Jack? Everybody knows that."

"Buddha. It's Buddha! Oprah Winfrey is nothing more than a common thief. She stole it from Buddha."

"Jack, I sense hostility. I think it's time you lived up to your failures."

"Oh good God, please. Do you know where I found you?"

"What if I didn't want to be found, Jack?"

"Then why did you do the sign?" He glanced over at what were now a floppy set of B-cups. "I was expecting maybe you were going to nick your finger or something."

"I'll tell you why, Jack. Because I am capital F freaking insane, Jack. Even I know that. And you know what else Jack? I like it."

Suzze looked over her shoulder without breaking her stride.

"You Shanghaied me, Jack."

"I did not Shanghai you."

"Kidnapped." Suzze looked over her shoulder again and picked up the pace, "Okay, enticed. Coerced. Bamboozled."

"I did not bamboozle anybody. I provided an opportunity."

Suzze turned to look back down the road, turned again and started walking even faster. The Old Man had trouble keeping up.

"You got a mean streak, Jack."

"Why do you say that?"

"Just cause, Jack. You're selling me short, Jack. Not a lot slips by me. Maybe you haven't figured that out yet, but you will. I can tell, Jack. I can just tell."

Suzze glanced over her shoulder again, panting, out of breath.

The mangy dog was trotting along now only five steps

behind.

What's with the dog, Jack?"

"He's just being a jerk."

Suzze froze in mid-stride and grabbed the Old Man by the back of his collar, jerking him back to her, "He? He? What? You know that dog, Jack? You want to talk about this, Jack? Think maybe we should open up with each other a little more, huh Jack? You don't talk much, do you Jack? I'm not happy, Jack. Let's establish that once and for all. You're not making me happy."

The Old Man reached into his pocket and pulled out another fungorum, presented it to Suzze and said, "Slow down. Be in the moment. Learn to revel in the passage of time."

He turned to stare down the mongrel until it stopped in its tracks, head bowed, tail between its legs. The dog turned, rear end facing Suzze and the Old Man, half-squatted and after straining and shaking violently, defecated in the middle of the road before trotting away, tail wagging.

Suzze popped the mushroom into her mouth, reached out her hand and wiggled her fingers, "Got any more, Jack?"

| Evolution

WHITE TEXT ROSE ACROSS MAGNIFICENT IMAGES from the Hubble Space Telescope, a universe that only God himself could have created. The words scrolled from bottom to top across the sixty-foot screen before disappearing into infinity.

Grammy Award-winning contemporary Christian singer Blessed Spunk delivered her version of the Lennon-McCartney tune, *You Say You Want An Evolution.*

It was the Evolutionist's Creed.

As Evolving Christians, we, with our hands to Heaven, attest that our Belief is not Belief alone. Our Principles are not our Faith. We cherish Science and Reason, which blesses us with a multitude of beneficial and necessary things. We trust nothing that contradicts our Belief, which, in all things is Supreme. We Desire and Pray, through our Benefactor, the Good and Gracious Steve, that God, in his infinite Generosity will grant magnificent things unto us. We Cherish free inquiry and the pursuit of Truth for the sake of Truth, with the unwavering Belief that no matter what mankind may accomplish on the Earth, no matter which Creeds may challenge us, our God is greater. We will Prevail.

Pastor Steve walked on stage, uncharacteristically serious, pensive, studious, as if uncertain of his next words.

He turned and glanced over his shoulder as the last words scrolled off the screen.

He shook his head, yes, yes indeed, that's who we are, that's what we stand for.

"Christians have been in charge of science since the beginning of time.

"Every great discovery? By a Christian.

"Yet today, we're told we don't know.

"We don't know science, they tell us.

"We can't understand. It's just too complicated, they say.

"The glories of the universe are hidden from us, unknowable by creatures as simple as we.

(Shake head in abject resignation)

"Poor, pitiful us. Just too stupid to understand anything.

"Yet they themselves will admit, sometimes, once in a while, that they don't know everything.

"But what they don't understand, we do.

"What they *can't* understand, we do.

"And that's what they don't understand.

"That they don't understand.

(Pause for reflection)

"Now, they say it's all probabilities.

"And you know what?

"They're right.

"It is all probabilities.

"Favor?

"How you will fare on this earth?

"That isn't fair.

"After all, who can know the mind of God?

"Who can know what God thinks is fair?

"Certainly not the scientists, blinded by their own ignorance.

"But they are right about one thing, it is all probabilities.

"It's all numbers.

"And who created the numbers?

(Point up)

"They say the earth, not just the earth, but everything we see, and do, and know, is all randomness, uncertainty.

"But who is in charge of uncertainty?

(With emphasis)

"Who else but God?

(Pause)

"They call it the Big Bang.

"And they're right.

"They are absolutely right."

Pastor Steve's energy visibly picks up. His feet do a little jig. His shoulders dance up and down in a rhythmic contrapunto. His hips wiggle. Inside, he's just busting to get loose.

"The Big Bang?

"THE BIG BANG!

(Slide across the stage, snap, stop, turn)

"Let me tell you about the Big Bang.

"My Lord *is* the Big Bang.

"He is big.

"He banged.

"And here we are.

(Shuffle across stage, hand on crotch, await applause)

"They just now figuring that out?

"I mean, thanks for the details science guys, but that's all you got?

"Details?

"Nothing wrong with details.

"But your details don't add up.

"Not for me.

"And not for you.

"AND NOT FOR GOD.

(Bam, bam, bam, drive it home, lighten up, go with humor, mime)

"Wait a minute.

"Wait a minute.

"Hold on.

"Hold on.

"I've got it.

"I got the answer right here."

Pastor Steve quick stepped frantically back and forth across the stage, punching imaginary numbers into an imaginary calculator, surprised at his imaginary results, entering the numbers again, surprised again, then pausing to look around the room before agreeing with himself.

"Yes," he shouted.

"I have the answer!

"God was right after all."

He gave the audience time to clap wildly and whistle and shout. Then he paused for his three count, looked to the floor, became pensive once again, searching for the next question, the next question he had rehearsed earlier in the front of the mirrors as he was being dressed.

"So let me 'splain it to you.

"It's simple.

"And the Lord God, in all his scientific wisdom created the Heavens and the Earth, and you and me, and everything therein.

"That was a long time ago.

"Who knows how long ago?

"Who cares?

"It's just a *detail*.

"So what's any different today?

"Nothin'.

"Sun still rises.

"Life goes on.

"God's in his heaven.

"All's right with the world.

(Muted applause)

"We don't have to know that something exists, or *how* it exists or why it exists, to know that GOD DID IT."

He walks across the stage, staring at the floor, admonishing the scientists of the world, "It's just a detail guys," shaking his head in the negative, "it's just a detail."

He lifts his arms in resignation, "Thanks for all the hard work and everything, but it's nothing special, no big deal."

He walks to the center of the stage, looks to the center of the auditorium and assumes his professorial demeanor again before concluding his lecture.

"Some people may make discoveries and know things before *you* do.

"That's okay.

"But it's nothing special.

"Because – and you can trust me on this one – nobody knows *anything* before God."

And then he shouts, at the same time glorifying those who understand and condemning those who question him, "BECAUSE IF YOU KNOW GOD, YOU KNOW EVERYTHING THERE IS TO KNOW."

The audience stands and screams in agreement.

(One, two, three, turn away, do not accept their applause, their applause is for the Lord, you are but his humble servant.)

(One, two, three, turn again to face them. Raise your arms to acknowledge their understanding and quiet them.)

(Look down. Count again, one, two, three. Raise your head and nod your agreement with what you are about to say.)

"IT'S JUST A DETAIL."

(Quietly now, just above a whisper)

"It's just a detail.

"And you know what they say, don't you?

"GOD IS IN THE DETAILS.

(Hold for applause)

"So, don't worry about it.

"Give all that you have to give and seek his favor.

"And then give some more.

"For is not God a jealous God?

"Flatter him.

"Bestow your blessings upon him and see his favor returned a hundred times.

"Now, that might happen.

"And it might not.

"Not here on earth.

(Point to the audience)

"Now God may take all that you have given and return it to someone you might think is unworthy.

"Don't worry about it.

"There's nothing you can do about it.

"It's not your decision to make.

"That's just God.

"That's just probabilities.

"And *that* is Evolution.

(Pause, reflect, point up)

"But what about up there?

"That's what you've got to worry about.

"So keep giving.

"Keep showing the Lord how you revere him.

"How you praise him.

"How you exalt him.

(Shake head in the affirmative.)

"Keep giving.

"And let God take care of the details."

Pastor Steve walked off stage, waving passively, with confidence and conviction and blessed reassurance, "It's what he does best."

The audience, realizing it had just heard six-thousand years, or six-billion years – What difference does it make? It's just a detail – of cosmic history explained logically, and with a clarity that only Pastor Steve was capable of elucidating, rose and chatted quietly among themselves, agreeing with each other that, well, yes, it was all just a detail, and that soon, the Lord would surely bestow his favor upon them.

Evolution, they called it.

Christian Evolution.

It was the Concept that had made the man they called Pastor Steve.

There was, however, one question that for most of them went unasked: Who had made Pastor Steve?

| Epicenter

Pudge was pressing his thumbs into Steven Hadad's Muladhara Chakra, located at the base of the spine on each side of the coccyx. The Muladhara is the root chakra where the main chakras, the Nadis, the Ida, the Pingala, and the Sushumna separate and course their way to the extremities. It is the most important chakra in the body, governing instinct, security, survival and basic human potentiality.

Pudge's fingers traced the Chakras from their source, as God might trace the Nile, following them here, where they converged at the center of the universe. All beauty, all meaning lay before him, clay beneath his hands.

As Pudge rotated his thumbs in circles, which had the effect of opening and closing Steve's butt cheeks, the holy man's sphincter would pop in and out of view, waxed, hairless.

To say Pudge's veneration of Pastor Steve's anal sphincter bordered on the devout would be an understatement. His recurring dream was to follow his muse, a faint, pink mole, so imperceptible that he doubted even Steve knew it was there, riding atop the sphincter ani externus, undulating up and down within the rolling puckers, so pale and pink and perfect in its symmetry that Pudge envisioned it circling in an elliptical orbit, gaining speed faster and faster until it slides into heaven, nirvana, paradise.

"Pudge?" Steve sensed that it was time to bring him back to

the here and now.

Pudge snapped to, "Overall, giving units are up point seven five. Toronto's up over two-fifty since incept. Canada was a good idea. Facial recognition just topped ninety-two percent. Payout's steady at forty-eight." He rattled off the numbers, mumbling to himself as much as to Pastor Steve. Pudge knew that although nothing in this life was certain, statistical analysis revealed truths otherwise hidden in seemingly random data. Nothing was meaningless if you had the vision to see across time and space. And Pudge could see it all, right down to the tenth of a decimal point, in his head.

And he knew he knew. Collections. Conversions. Attendance. Attritions. Pudge knew. Others knew something. Pudge knew all. He was the one. And right now he was wishing, hoping maybe for an attaboy, or a meaningful question, or at least a supportive comment.

"It can all get a little boring if you want to know the truth." Steve pinched his buttocks momentarily pushing Pudge's fingers away.

"Those whom the gods wish to destroy, they first make bored," said Pudge.

"Yeah. Whatever."

"We should start thinking about adding another bank," Pudge offered. "Maybe Tatas. Their Global Finance would be a good match."

Steve grunted.

To Williford Ransom, he and Steven Hadad were one and the same, spawn of a common homunculus, each with his own corporeal existence, but of a single spirit, not only homoiousios, of a similar substance, but homoousios, of the same substance, the single iota that decreed God the Father and God the Son to be one and the same, as Williford was to Steve, the precursor, the creator, the impetus, Pudge the life-force, Steve the shepherd, guiding their flock to a higher level, building their kingdom here on Earth as it is to be in Heaven.

Pastor Steve, on the other hand, didn't sweat the details. In his world it was simple. He was the talent. Pudge was the bookkeeper.

Pudge didn't quite see it that way. Especially since Steven Hadad wouldn't know an algorithm if it were sliding up his ass, as Pudge's thumb was autonomously tempting to do right now. But Pudge, as always, avoided the temptation, all temptation.

He turned his attention to the back of his hand. He gouged at a scab. Just enough to loosen it. Just enough to draw blood. When the drop grew large enough that it risked running off his hand, he let the scab drop back, capturing the blood, holding it in place. Tomorrow it would be bigger still, big enough to consume, to roll across his tongue, to shred between his teeth, the raw-iron taste of his essence re-entering his body, giving him strength.

"How are Becky and the kids?" Pudge asked. He noticed an involuntary pucker.

"Maybe not the best move I ever made," Steve mumbled toward the floor.

"Did not the apostle Paul teach that it is well for a man not to touch a woman?" Pudge questioned, rhetorically.

"Bambinos, Pudge. Heirs apparent. Family values. A domestic front end representing our metaproduct. Your idea, by the way."

Pudge didn't like to take the blame for anything, especially when the blame was his and his alone.

"The coloring books were a good idea," Steve said, making

no point in particular.

"Give me a child," Pudge replied, again quoting his spiritual mentor, Saint Paul. "Donations to youth ministries up eleven and a half percent." (Pastor Steve was on every page of the coloring book, along with his friend Jesus, leading his little lambs to the path of righteousness, their parents toward direct deposit.)

"Shame about Joel," Steve said, with no hint of emotion.

"Suzze?" asked Pudge.

"Cutie Pootie? Fucked up, buddy. That's all I've got to say. Maybe I'll give her a call. Hit it again for old time's sake." Steve's voice bounced off the floor and back to Pudge.

Pudge contained his anger at hearing Suzze's name and turned his focus back to the mole. Small. Pink. To Pudge, it appeared as a slight imperfection on an otherwise perfect visage. He fixed his gaze upon it. Could it indeed be imperfect, imperfection on an otherwise flawless being? He wondered if anyone else had ever seen it. Did Steven know it was there, hidden away as it was? He extended his finger and approached it cautiously, uncertain, afraid of what might happen, either the horrible ugliness it might reveal, or the ecstasy he might feel. He resisted, and resistance was good, and he was proud of himself for having done so.

"Suzze Woozy," Steve mumbled under his breath.

"Jezebel," snapped Pudge.

"Where there's chaos, there's opportunity."

Pudge's fingers grew rigid, tense. Not now. Leave it be.

Pudge lowered his head so that he was only inches from Steve's backside, paused, struggled, then rose up, resisting the urge to absorb Steve's pheromones into his own homoiousios, fighting his fingers as they involuntarily crept toward his nose.

"Roll over," he said.

- - -

Missy Swiegel and her husband, the Reverend Ezekiel Swiegel of Zeke Swiegel Teleministries International, were having afternoon drinks and otherwise socializing on the veranda of their Naples, Florida winter home when Mrs. Swiegel noticed the Reverend's stomach growl in an abnormally loud fashion, followed by a burp and a broad smile. Mrs. Swiegel believed that the Reverend was merely smiling at the comfort he felt having just attained digestive relief. She continued to lightly converse with him but to no response. Miffed, she went inside to ask her housekeeper, Betsy Lee, to prepare another Peach Daiquiri for herself and a Tom Collins, light on the gin, for the Reverend, as his was losing its frost.

She returned to find the Reverend sitting in the same position as she had left him, his big smile still present, the only difference being that something that appeared to be scrambled eggs was oozing out of the corners of his mouth. Mrs. Swiegel assumed it to be the morning's breakfast but noticed whatever it was, was loose and runny and that the Reverend preferred his eggs well done, and that Betsy Lee knew that as well, and always prepared his eggs well done or hard boiled depending on his preference at the time.

Betsy Lee delivered the drinks and sat the Tom Collins -- light on the gin -- in front of the Reverend, expecting him to down the first half in one gulp as was his custom. When he did not do so, Mrs. Swiegel conferred with Betsy Lee who thought it wise to call an ambulance.

Swiegel was pronounced dead at the scene by EMS, apparently from massive head injuries.

Upon hearing from EMS that Mr. Swiegel was deceased, Mrs. Swiegel commented that she knew he must be in Heaven, having passed away peacefully and with a smile on his face, praise Jesus.

Mrs. Swiegel is being detained for questioning.

Authorities are awaiting autopsy results before commenting further.

| Il Messaggero

YESHU'A BAR YOSEF WAS HAVING AN EARLY SUPPER.

He was sitting in the courtyard of his favorite restaurant, Piperno, on Monte dé Cenci, in the now-fashionable Jewish quarter, a neighborhood that had once been the Ghetto of Rome.

He was reading *Il Messaggero*. Yeshu'a was old school. He liked the feel of paper in his hands. He snapped and folded the newspaper, first in half, then in quarters, then in eighths, keeping it small and unobtrusive.

Normally, the Ristorante Piperno would object if a guest were so bold as to read a newspaper, or a book, or anything for that matter, while dining, even outside. One did nothing to detract oneself from one's enjoyment of one's food. But the evening was young, most of their guests wouldn't appear before nine at the earliest, and Yeshu'a was a regular, and, well, special.

A waiter, his waiter, appeared, suggesting a bottle of Incisa della Rocchetta Sassicaia, which, of course, met his approval, for Yeshu'a was an agreeable man, famously easy to please, especially when it came to wine. And, at only €150 a bottle, about two-hundred American dollars, it was fairly priced. (How he despised 'Euros' and yearned for the old days, when life's pleasures were measured in Lira. Oh well, the past is the past.) And, since all that was required of him was to sign the chit, it was of no concern, the accounting fell to someone else.

The waiter poured the wine, nodded a bright *buon appetito* and silently went his way without further conversation.

Yeshu'a was dining light, his stomach upset. The news. How he despised the news. Everything changing, rarely for the better.

The Vatican was bankrupt. Yet another pathetic American had visited heaven, this time having taken his French poodle. And the poodle had written a book, insisting that indeed, all dogs do go to heaven. Americans! They were even considering a movie.

Now there was a cookbook, a cookbook for heaven. Food, clothing, automobiles, nothing, it seemed, could be sold unless it was endorsed by God himself.

Another preacher, barely literate, had acquired another sinfully expensive aircraft, no doubt to fly to heaven himself, spend the weekend and report back to his flock, the episode good for another million or so in donations.

Another had buried his poor mother in an amusement park beside a talking cow. How was it that cows talk? Vile demagogue. Did shame know no limits?

And now, The New and Improved Testament! Who were these liars? These cheats? These charlatans?

"Thou shalt not bear false witness," he said aloud.

"*Mi scusi signore?* Excuse me sir?" the waiter asked.

"Oh nothing Tommaso, just talking to the paper."

The waiter placed a plate of olives and a small pagnotta of bread before him and topped off his wine. Yeshu'a's glass never ran empty. Soon, the waiter returned with a plate of Carciofi alla Guidia, artichokes in the Jewish style, a serving for two, for Yeshu'a was a glutton for artichokes in season. They were presented alongside an assortment of cheeses, favoring pecorino and parmigiano, rather common he knew but his favorites nonetheless. Why try to improve upon perfection? was the rule he lived by.

It was an altogether delightful evening, like every evening in Rome, but his poor stomach would not leave him alone.

The religious wars in America were heating up, sure to spill over into the rest of the world if something wasn't done to stop them.

He loved Rome. It was a cozy town. It was home.

But perhaps, he thought, as he tore off a piece of bread and sopped up the oil from the artichokes, perhaps John was right. Perhaps it was time to move on.

- - -

Taking their marketing strategy to the next level, Goldwater and Cruze segmented what was becoming known as the Dis-Xy demographic (disenfranchised exceptional youth) with a message that encompassed all three major religions in the United States.

Billboards were copy-tested in selected markets and targeted high-education, low-income males 18-34, who were deemed to be the most aggressive of their cohort and most inventive in their ability to bilk the system. The copy on the billboards read: Have You Been Sexually Mutilated by a Christian, a Muslim, or a Jew? Beneath that was an 800 number and the web address, www.goldwaterandcruze.com/foreskin.

Two images were tested.

The first was a cucumber with the end cut off.

The second was the same shot of the sliced cucumber, but with a Wüsthof paring knife in frame.

The image with the knife tested 88% more effective than the image of the cucumber alone, a clear winner and the shot they ran with.

Jewish pediatricians were initially targeted, with a seemingly unlimited supply of "non-practicing" unemployed former Jewish men eager to cash in.

The response rate was wholly unanticipated and compelled Goldwater and Cruze to add 47 more attorneys in offices throughout the United States.

Episode 3

He Comes

Preview

Scenes

| Amazing Grace

LISA WAS SITTING ON A BOXY GREEN COUCH.

It had once been chartreuse. Now, after years of human effluvia had ground into the cushions it was a dingy olive drab. A matching club chair sat directly in front of it. There was a chrome and Formica desk several feet behind the chair.

Lisa picked at a loose thread where the edge of a cushion had worn through. She had been here before. Many times. Drab. Drab, drab, drab.

She slipped off her hospital-white canvas moccasins and put her bare feet on the edge of the sofa and dropped her knees to her sides. Lisa was limber. Flexible. Skinny as a rail. She lifted the elastic band to her gray sweatpants and looked between her legs, then reached behind and pulled the pants tight up the crack of her ass so that a petite, hairy little camel toe bulged through. She reached under her T-shirt, twisted her nipples and then pulled the shirt tight under her arms until they poked out, razor sharp.

The door opened and the shrink walked in. New guy. No surprise.

There had been a half a dozen others before him.

She was ready.

She had changed the story every time, not because she was crazy, which she was not, but because if the truth didn't work the first time, she figured another version of the truth might stand a better chance with the next guy.

It was just a matter of telling them what they wanted to hear, these chicken-shit little dweebs with their masters of social work degrees. MSW, CNS, LPL, NCC, DCC, CHT, the more letters they stuck behind their names the more full of shit they were. Flunkies not smart enough to make it into med school. Government-issue, dickless little Dr. Phils.

She played them. She could feel their breath quicken when she made a sexual remark, see them blush when she told her story, whatever her story was at the time.

Of course, they pretended not to believe her. They didn't have to. Why should her truth count? Even after one of them, that four-eyed, kinky-headed little asshole, crawled up on top of her and they caught him. Even after they caught him they didn't believe her. She imagined she might enjoy it – joke on him. Joke on her, the pencil-dicked little weasel came before he could get it inside. All over the couch, for Christ's sake. She looked down to see if she could find the spot. Call me Dr. Randy, he had said to her earlier that day. All of them were Dr. First Name Only. Dr. Bob. Dr. Rob. Dr. Bill. Dr. Phil. Dr. Kiss My Ass, worthless sons of bitches.

This one was no different. He sat there, saying nothing, testing her, wondering if she would go first.

She didn't. Wasn't going to. Don't give anything away. Not for free.

He flipped through her file, stopped and read out loud:

Watch your thoughts, for they become words.
Watch your words, for they become actions.
Watch your actions, for they become habits.

Watch your habits, for they become character.
Watch your character, for it becomes your destiny.

"That's very nice. You write that?"

"Guess I'm a poet and didn't even know it."

The shrink knew, of course, that she was intentionally and sarcastically lowering herself to his level with her vapid comment. And he knew she didn't write it. He'd seen it on the Internet, unattributed. Still, quoting this verse showed amazing clarity, perhaps maturity. This girl, strike that, this woman got it, finally, far better than most.

He continued to flip through the file, obviously the first time he had seen it.

She continued to size him up. Older guy. Wedding ring. Good suit, once upon a time. Ratty now. Worn. Poor guy, maybe he used to be somebody. A big shot. Fallen from grace? Maybe. Malpractice? Screwing little boys? Caught sneaking into patient rooms in the middle of the night? Wonder if he can still get it up? Wonder if he comes too soon.

Dr. Jerkoff sucked snot, hacked and swallowed it with a loud gulp as he continued to flip through the file.

Cigarette stains on his fingers. She could smell it on his clothes. Play him for daddy. Poor, pitiful me. Whatever. Just get this fucking show on the road. She'd rather be back in her room or listening to those assholes in group whine than sit here waiting for Mr. College Professor to speak.

He found what he was looking for. 168. Smart girl. Too smart for her own good. Too smart for anybody's good.

He closed the file. Looked at her. Said nothing. Looked away. Looked back, watching her begin to squirm. He waited a few seconds more until he could see that she was trying to quit squirming but could not, which told him he was in control.

He sucked more snot, reached into his pocket and squirted decongestant into each nostril with a loud, nasty snort and said, "Why don't you cut the bullshit and just tell me what happened?"

It took her a minute to figure out what to do. She stared back, snorted her own make believe snot in response, thought what-the-fuck and started to talk.

"It started when I was eleven, exactly when I had my first period. I had an older sister Tina, who hadn't started hers, even though she was three years older which meant I blew it for both of us. Periods are bad, can't be a girl anymore. Before that, she would dress us up like little ballerinas or cowgirls and we'd go around to the neighbors' houses, she being my mom, Betty Jean. We'd sing and dance and tell them all how much we loved Jesus. At the time we're living with the millionaires in a gated (Lisa flicked her fingers to make air quotes) community, neighbors mostly crooked car dealers, bank people, stock brokers, financial guys like my dad. People you don't really want to be around unless you're my mom. Big shits was all she ever wanted to be. My dad thought it would be good for his career. Looks matter. Got to look like the rest of them. I mean, I understand. For him, that was probably right. But shit, man, you got to be who you are. And him and my mom. They just spent all their time fucking each other over. And I don't mean in a good way. He was a chief financial guy for somebody. In the end, they fucked him out of his job and he moved to a small house in an old neighborhood downtown. Started doing rentals. Buy it. Fix it up. Be your own boss. Women love that swarthy, work with your hands type. Took up skydiving. Triathlon. Motorcycle but not a Harley. The whole nine yards man. The life he always wanted. Good for him. Good for him. Get away from Betty Jean. Catch up on his fuck time. Lots of young babes. Only he killed my sister. Tina."

The shrink continued to flip through his papers. She waited for him to stop, maybe pay her some attention. He didn't.

"Betty Jean's a trip. A sad, fat, scared little woman who can't live unless she's one of them and she knows that no matter what she does, they're never going to let her be one of them. But she keeps trying the only way she knows how, to out-Jesus them. Looks just like Tammy Faye Bakker. No shit. Hair. Makeup. Build. Right down to the goofy clothes and cheap jewelry. Sick bitch.

"So it's a while later and Tina gets her period. Then she got pregnant. First time she gets laid, she gets pregnant. What kind of luck is that?

"Couldn't get an abortion. Too young to do it on her own and Betty Jean wouldn't sign for it.

"Dad wouldn't let her live with him. They'd separated by then, remember. Betty Jean and us, me and Tina, we're still in the big house. Time for her to take responsibility for her actions. Actions have consequences. That's what he said.

"They decided on some Christian home. Stay there. Give it up for adoption. Tina didn't want to give up her baby. Get rid of it, yeah, maybe. But give it over to some sick fuck Jesus freak? No way. No way she would do that.

"Took her to a shrink. At least that's what she said she was. That big fucking church on the south side. What kind of church needs a psychiatrist?

"Troubled girl. That's what they decided. Bullshit. Tina was the straightest, kindest, gentlest, smartest person I ever knew. Yeah, she was troubled. But it was Betty Jean's trouble she was living, not her own. Betty Jean decided it was Satan made her do it. Tina looked like an angel. Small. White skin. Blond hair with those little pin curls in front. Reddish-blond. Strawberry blond. Looked just like that painting of Venus standing on a seashell. The one Botticelli did. Just like her. I got that poster. Not a poster. A picture. At least I had it until that bitch Betty Jean shit-canned it. Me and Tina tore it out of a book. We put it up on the wall in my bedroom. After they were asleep, Tina would come in and get in the bed and we'd look at it and I'd joke about how much it looked like Tina except that she didn't have boobies, and, you know, just silly little girl shit but that stopped the day she died. Never understood what that had to do with it really, but I guess the lesson I learned is that shit doesn't have to make sense. Just what some ignorant asshole wants to make up in her mind. I loved my sister. I loved my sister. If I could kill somebody and bring her back, I'd do it in a heartbeat, don't you fucking doubt it. I miss Tina. Fucking Satan. Give me a break."

The shrink looked up with a Why-did-you-stop? look on his face without saying anything.

Lisa picked her nose, pulled out a wad of snot, rolled it between her fingers and flicked it across the room.

"So Tina got a fake I.D."

"It says here she jumped"

"Yeah, but this was before. When she was still pregnant. And she didn't jump.

"So Tina got a fake I.D. Said she was eighteen. She was almost sixteen anyway so she almost looked the part. She still looked young, always did. But she was close enough to pull it off. Started dancing. Goddamn, she did make the money. The more she showed her belly, the more her belly showed, the more they paid. She was thin, kind of skinny, maybe too skinny then, so it took her a long time to show big. The guys who owned the bar, they all knew she was pregnant but they couldn't say for sure. Maybe. Maybe not. Some kind of law maybe, you can't show your tits if you're pregnant, can't slide your ass up and down a pole if you're knocked up. Wouldn't surprise me. Then when she really got her belly, the nipples, you know how the nipples get big and flat and brown? When that happened they told her not to come back. Couldn't take the chance. Maybe they would get busted or something, I don't know. So she started doing private dances. Still making money, I guess, but she wouldn't talk about it. What she did then. She wouldn't talk about it at all. Only did it for a couple of weeks, sleeping in her car. Then she left."

"Left where?"

"Left. It came on the news. Mom always watched that stuff, reality shows, crap like that and they broke in with live exclusive breaking eyewitness news. They didn't have a camera there. It was really just a feed from a bunch of iPhones they'd tapped into but there she was, Tina dancing high up on the edge of a parking deck downtown.

"Dad was with us. In the big house. Visiting. Paying the bills or some shit like that. He snatched me by the arm and we were out the door. Just a few minutes, we didn't live too far, eight or ten blocks, a half a mile maybe, not even that much. I was still in my pajamas. I didn't understand it at the time but now it makes sense. Maybe he thought I could talk her down. A hundred people there at least, everybody recording. Everybody going ooh and aah. Most of them loaded, jacked up, bar hopping. Somebody said the cops were going to Taze her.

"I looked up and she saw me and she looked down at me

and smiled. And then she flew. Right off the edge with her arms stretched out, just hovering up there like a bird, like a beautiful white bird with her nightgown fluttering in the wind. And I said don't stop, don't stop, keep flying, you can do it, don't stop, just fly away, just go, please, please, please don't stop, just go. But she couldn't do it anymore."

The shrink's palms were together, resting in front of his face. He looked up.

"And when she hit, everybody ran away from her. You know how, in the movies and on TV everybody runs up and wants to see? No. They all ran away, like they were going to catch something. Like it was contagious.

"The cops and the ambulance people, they put a sheet over her and then they just all stood around like they didn't know what to do next.

"And then she rose up, up through the sheet and she looked at me and she was glowing and she just floated there above the ground with her arms out like she was feeling the air and feeling free. And she rose up some more and stopped, like she was waiting, or didn't want to go on. And I looked at her and I said, go, go, please go. Don't stop. Just go.

"And then she floated up some more, higher, like smoke and she stopped again and looked down where she had been, and then the little one rose up too and they just kept rising up together until they were high, high up, until they disappeared until all you could see was the stars.

"And I was ready to go home."

The shrink sat back, hacked and spit it into a wad of Kleenex.

Lisa looked over at the door, thinking maybe she'd make a run for it.

"What happened after that?" The shrink was staring at her, eye to eye.

Lisa lifted up off the couch to pull her pants out of the crack of her ass, readjusted herself and put her feet back on the floor. She lay forward with her head between her knees staring at her toes.

She looked up. "After that? After that, the shit hit the fan.

"After that Betty Jean went from being just an average crazy nut bag to a completely out of control Jesus freak."

She sat bolt upright and leaned back with both arms stretched across the back of the sofa.

"Then it was my turn. In Betty Jean's mind, it made sense that after Satan got finished with Tina, he'd come for me next. Makes sense if you know Betty Jean. She fed me to those cocksuckers.

"I'd started hanging out with what everybody called the Goths only we didn't call ourselves that. Didn't call ourselves anything. Just hung out. All black. Mostly black anyway. Fake tattoos, not old enough to get the real thing. We'd pierce each other. Stick in whatever was laying around. Draw weird symbols on your arms with different colored ball point pens. Poets and artists, hanging out at the mall. I was the fashion designer. No drugs. Maybe a hit off a joint sometimes. No sex. Jerked a guy off a couple of times. So what? Black fingernails.

"Betty Jean couldn't stand it. She'd shriek, squeal, speak in tongues. What a fucking trip that was, like she was learning a foreign language or something. She'd walk around the house practicing, jubba, jubba, jubba, hoodie, hoodie, hoodie. All this religious shit with her was just a fad, jump from one to the other looking for something that fit. Then she got all into the gospel of prosperity. Prosperity. She'd say it in this goofy way like that crazy fuck on TV. *Pros-perity.* How Jesus wanted her to have *pros-perity* and how if she just believed it would be delivered unto her. Like Jesus drives the fucking UPS truck, you know what I mean? Started buying shit all this crazy shit because Jesus wanted her to have it. That shit's on TV. All day long. And these crazy bitches believe it. Ran up her credit card. Dad's credit card. He put a stop to that.

"She was still going to Covenant, the big pink cathedral. Ten-thousand people. What kind of sick fuck goes to a pink church? Dad had quit. No church. New girlfriend, all spiritual and shit, smoking pot, happy, at least he looked happy to me. Who knows?

"So anyway, back to me and Satan. So, Betty Jean had them come for me, these crazy sons of bitches from Covenant. I was in my room. The door opened and there they were, big smiles. Bunch of young dudes. White shirts. Black pants. One to drive the car. One to hold the bible and pray while they walked my ass out the door. Why fight it? What you gonna do? Honestly, I thought I could outsmart them. Reason with them or argue with them or convert them, change their minds. Flipped Betty Jean the bird on the way out. Like that's gonna do any good.

"I knew better. Got to the pink pile of shit. They were waiting for me. Standing in the middle of a room. I guess in the basement. No windows, couldn't tell for sure. A bunch of those little halogen track lights shining on top of me.

"Four or five of them. Older. Pasty white. Fat fucks. Dressed just like the younger guys. White shirts, clip-on ties. Walking around me in circles. Couple of them had a bible. One reading scripture. One praying or whatever they call that shit where they just look up and go yes Jesus, thank you Jesus, praise you Jesus, boogie, boogie, Jesus. And every time one would circle in front of you, he'd ask you a question, like some kind of crazy-assed musical chairs or a merry-go-round. On and on and on until you couldn't hold out anymore. Give them what they want. Tell them what they want to hear and get the fuck out.

"Yes, I know.
"Yes, I know.
"Yes, I understand.
"Yes, I accept Jesus Christ as my Lord and Savior.
"Yes, I pray for his divine love and mercy.
"Yes, I will honor my father and mother.
"Yes, I will remember the Sabbath and keep it holy.
"Yes, Jesus.
"Yes, Jesus.
"Thank you, Jesus.
"Yes, Jesus.
"Yes, yes, yes, yes, yes, yes.

"On and on and on and fucking on until you just gave up.

"They walked me out to the lobby. Big smiles on their faces. One still had his hardon. Ran to the bathroom to jerk off.

"Betty Jean was waiting. Big smile. Everything's going to be alright from now on. She could just tell, thank you Jesus.

"I didn't want to kill her. I didn't even hate her. I felt sorry for her. Pitied her. Talk about a woman who couldn't wipe her own ass without someone else's approval.

"On the way home, we drove past this wood church, like you see on a postcard or a puzzle. Drove by it all the time. Betty Jean would just swoon and go on about how cute it was and how she'd like for us to go there someday but it was a colored church and she just wasn't sure what they would think, they being who I don't know, somebody whose approval she thought she needed. We drove past it a hundred times and every time she'd say the same goddamned thing. I was already sick of hearing it and this was the last night I was going to hear it ever again.

"Got home, Betty Jean had new pink and blue pajamas with baby Jesus holding a lamb and little baby angels and shit like that that she had bought for me just for this special occasion.

"Looked in the closet. All my clothes were gone. Most of them I'd designed and made myself. My grandmother, dad's mom, she gave me this sewing machine. Bought my own fabric. Made my own clothes. Sometimes I'd go to Goodwill. Cut up two or three different outfits and sew them back together, accessorize them with scarves and plastic jewels. Started out looking like Stevie Nicks. Everybody laughed. Ended up Elvira. I liked that. Making your own clothes. It's fun."

Lisa paused to lean forward again and pick at her shoes.

She glanced up, meeting the shrink eye to eye waiting for him to blink. He didn't.

She talked to the floor, her voice low and flat. "I crawled out the window, barefoot, still in those pajamas. I was out of it. You know how that works sometimes? You're completely fucking out of it but man you're focused. All that matters is right in front of you. Just do it. Do it or go fucking crazy. Make it happen. Now. Right fucking now.

"I walked to the Quick Stop, bought a can of lighter fluid and a pack of matches. Got the matches because they were free. Should have bought a lighter. Wasn't thinking. Walked back to the church. Only a mile or two. Not far.

"It was summer, the middle of summer, hot, sticky even in the middle of the night. It was this little narrow road. It was not like a big church or anything. Paint peeling. All wood. There was like a bare light bulb in one of those old-timey fixtures hanging over the front door, bugs flying around it, a pile of dead bugs laying on the step. No stained glass. Just regular windows painted with that white stuff that you can see halfway through. They had just cut the grass. Smelled like watermelon."

Lisa looked up without raising her head, her voice suddenly perky, "You know the only thing I ever asked for in this place? The only thing? The one, little, special thing I always wanted that would have made it a little more bearable? Watermelon. I love watermelon. Baloney and Jell-O. That's what you get here. Gag a maggot."

A secretary came in, unannounced, and handed the shrink a form. He looked it over and nodded. She left.

Lisa sat up, looking from side to side, mumbling, "So I went around back, out of the light. I went around to the back so that nobody could see me from the road. Squirted the lighter fluid on the door. Struck a match. Nothing. Fizzled out. Did it again. Same thing. Found an old newspaper under the steps, packed it in the crack under the door, squirted the rest of the lighter fluid, stuck a match to it. Nothing. I folded the pack of matches into a little tent and struck them all at once. A little smoke. That's all. Went out. Fuck me, you know?

"So I was walking home, about halfway there, the fire trucks come screaming by. Shit. No way. Couldn't be. But I got scared and started running. My anger high had worn off. Couldn't be. But it was. If I hadn't been running down the road in the middle of the night in those fucking pink and blue pajamas, they probably wouldn't have noticed me. I made it home, to Betty Jean's, back through the window, back in the bed. Nothing. Nothing happened.

"Next day, it was all over the news. Betty Jean couldn't get over it. Couldn't stop talking about it. Like it was her very own church. Her special place. Who could do such a thing? Yada-yada-yada.

"Then, two days later, they showed up. Had it all figured out. Those fucking pajamas, fucking pink and blue pajamas. Guys on the fire truck couldn't help but notice, know what I mean? People say, what were you thinking? That's the point. I wasn't thinking.

"And the rest, as they say, is history."

The shrink looked up from the file. "Where's Betty Jean now?"

"House trailer. Dad quit paying on the big house. Fuck her. I don't know if they sold it or if it was foreclosed.

"Came to see me right after that. I was here by then. Up on the third floor. Still in lockdown. She had a new boyfriend, some joker named Paul Wayne something or another. She'd say his name like it was one word. PauWayne. PauWayne this. PauWayne that. Short, like her. Snaggle-toothed. Poofed up hair full of hairspray. So dad cut her off completely then. Betty Jean's screwed. Probably hopped up on a zillion antidepressants.

"Anyway, I'm lying there, up on the third in restraints and Paul Wayne's kneeling by the bed reading this shit from his bible. Betty Jean won't shut the fuck up, both of them talking at the same time. If I could have chewed my arm off and gotten loose, I'd a ripped the bitch's throat out.

"He'd been laid off, plant closed down, couldn't get a job, so she had to start working at Walmart. Never had a job in her life that I remember. How she ever got a job at Walmart is beyond me."

"Are you going to go back there? When you get out, are you going to go back there?"

"You got to be shittin' me."

"Just asking."

"I don't know. I don't know where I'll go. Back with my dad, maybe. At least he's sane."

"Do you need for me to call someone?"

"Why?"

"Someone to pick you up. We called your mother. And your dad. Several times but they never called back."

"Pick me up? You mean I'm outta here?"

"Yeah."

"When?"

"Now. Right now." He was signing a paper. "You're discharged. Go. Have a beautiful life."

She decided against asking any more questions, didn't want to push her luck.

"You can wait here. You can call somebody. In fact, we prefer that you do. You can't just walk out. You need to call someone. Or we'll do it for you. And stop by the front desk on the way out. They'll give you some money, not much, bus fare."

She stood up and walked to the door.

"Lisa!"

He snapped apart a form and handed her the pink copy. "Your papers. You'll need them. Sooner or later."

She took the paper and looked down at him, wondering if she should say thank you or something. Maybe give him a hug.

"Lisa, come back. Sit down for a minute."

She propped on the arm of the sofa, making a point of not making herself comfortable.

"Don't you see, Lisa? Nobody cares about you. Nobody cares what you think. Or how you feel. Not your mother. Not your father. Nobody here. Nobody cares about you at all. Learn to live with that and you'll do just fine. If not, you'll end up right back here. Or someplace worse."

She stood again and walked towards the door, determined not to let anything stop her this time.

"Lisa." She heard him suck snot, swallow it and say again, "Lisa?"

"Yes," she said without turning.

"Lisa?"

"Yes?" She paused, holding her breath.

"Happy birthday."

She smiled, walked out the door, did not run, walked quickly back to her room, grabbed her Hello Kitty backpack, which she had always kept packed and ready to go and only then started running down the hall to catch the elevator before the door closed. She thought about stopping downstairs for bus fare, changed her mind, decided not to wait for the elevator and ran down the stairs, out the door and halfway across the parking lot before she finally stopped to get her bearings.

She realized she didn't know his name. The shrink. No idea. She looked around, snorted some imaginary snot, hacked it up and spit it out. Good fucking bye.

Eighteen years old today and free as a bird.

Maybe.

Maybe not.

| The Garden

"EVER DROP ACID?"

They were in a valley. The sun was shining. The birds were tweeting. Flowers bloomed. Bees buzzed. The breeze fluttered through Suzze's hair.

"Jesus, Jack, don't tell me you're tripping again."

Suzze wandered along the bank of a picture-perfect pond, fingering the flora and fauna. Cattails. Dragonflies. Tadpoles. Everything sparkled like a pixilated image.

"That's what this place reminds me of," said the Old Man. "A real trip. Like one of those Thomas Kinkade prints where everything glitters and glistens. They used to sell them by the side of the road."

"I know what they are, Jack. I owned the definitive collection. And mine were originals, not cheesy roadside prints."

"Used to? What happened to them?"

Suzze didn't want to explain and changed the subject.

"I got a headache, Jack. A migraine. At least I think it's a migraine. Never had them before. Been getting them a lot lately."

"Like your head's going to explode?"

"Not funny, Jack. You're not good at funny, Jack. Some people are good at funny. You're not. Don't mean to hurt your feelings or anything but you're not, that's all."

Suzze pulled off a cattail, peeled away the wool and held it up to blow in the wind.

"Is all this real, Jack?"

"Looks real to me."

"You know what I mean. Is it *real* real or have you made me hallucinate?"

The Old Man shrugged, "Everything is as real as you want it to be."

"I've heard better pick up lines from sixteen-year-old boys, Jack."

Suzze blew the last wooly seeds from the cattail.

The Old Man lay back in the grass.

Suzze scratched her crotch.

"This wandering in the wilderness, Jack. Am I supposed to be learning something? Some metaphysical, spiritual growth and enlightenment thing? Because, if I am, it's not working. All I'm getting is more constipated."

She broke off a blade of grass and stretched it between her thumbs to make a Jew's harp. *Bump-bah-dah-dah-dah, dah, bump-da-bump-bump.* She was trying to play the riff to *In a Gadda da Vida* but realized that even she couldn't recognize what it was supposed to be. A musician, she was not. Oh well.

The Old Man sat up, perked up, and crossed his legs. "I have a story for you."

"I like stories, Jack. Tell me a story."

The Old Man took a breath to collect his thoughts and began, "There was a Greek philosopher…"

Suzze stood up and stuck her toe in the water.

"His name was Epicurus."

"Whose name was Epicurious, Jack?"

"The Greek. The philosopher."

"You know what I liked most about being a Christian, Jack?"

"*Liked?* As in past tense?"

"What I liked most about being a Christian was how dirty it was. All that sexual repression stuff. Now I feel all...," Suzze did an exaggerated shudder, "...all clean."

The Old Man waited, hoping she would run out of steam.

"I miss being perverted, Jack. I don't feel perverted any more. It was fun, Jack. Sometimes."

"So this Greek philosopher..."

She started to walk around the pond. "Maybe I need to get laid."

"So there was this Greek philosopher..."

"Epicurious." Suzze stopped beside the trunk of a deformed, gangly tree, half in, half out of the water, shaking it as if testing it for strength.

The Old Man spoke louder, not sure if she was paying him any attention, "At about that time, people were beginning to learn about science..."

"I don't think I can do that anymore."

"What?"

"Be a Christian."

"Okay, let's move on. *So there was...*"

"But I did like it. Dirty, dirty, dirty." Suzze slid her right foot onto the lowest branch which hung low out over the pond, sometimes out of the water, sometimes just dipping under the surface. It was covered with moss, slippery. She was feeling adventurous.

"Back then, scientists were called natural philosophers..."

"Say that again, Jack." Suzze slid out onto the branch, concentrating on her balance, inch by inch, one foot following the other.

"Natural philosophers. Back then, scientists were called natural philosophers…"

The branch wobbled as Suzze stood up straight with her arms outstretched to keep her balance.

"So back then, scientists were called natural philosophers, and even then, people doubted the existence of God."

Like a sideways tightrope walker, Suzze inched her way out the branch, just inches above the water. Having mastered the branch, she spread her legs, lifted her robe and squatted down.

The Old Man decided to substitute loud for serious, now half shouting, "So now the Greeks had a choice. Which would it be? Science or God?"

Plop.

Still loud, "So Epicurus said, 'Better to follow the Myths about the Gods than to become a Slave to the Destiny of Natural Philosophers.' "

Plop.

"Are you with me on this?" asked the Old Man.

Plunk.

"Got it, Jack. God or science, the eternal struggle."

Plink.

Suzze watched her deposits return to the ecosystem with fascination. She called them her *Little Oprahs* and watched, one by one as they plinked and plunked and plopped into the water swirling to line up with the gentle current on their journey to who knows where.

Seeing that his lecture was getting him nowhere, he decided to cut to the point, "The point is, Epicurus thought it better to live a life in harmony with Nature, and with God, than to spend your life in a cubicle, a cog in the wheel of free market capitalism."

"I'm with you, Jack."

One by one, bolus by bolus, she launched them.

She reached over and snapped off a twig with a leaf still attached and poked it into one of her creations. She arched her back and raised her right hand to her forehead and saluted, "I christen thee, HMS Joel Osmond," before leaning down to blow on the sail and send it on its way.

Next, there was a canoe.

Then a kayak.

Then, *The Doctor Oz*, a sleek, streamlined sailing vessel to be sure.

And lastly, with some effort, a giant. A cruise ship, an ocean liner, *Her Majesty Queen Oprah*.

There were no warships.

No battleships.

No destroyers.

No aircraft carriers.

But as she watched, one did sink. Why would it sink? A submarine, maybe? As she watched it descend beneath the surface, a large, spotted goldfish swam up, his nose just breaking the surface of the water. He, or it, bobbed out of the water, then sank just beneath the surface again. The fish came back, nose poking out of the water, and nudged a little higher, brushing the hair between her legs, which hung down in amber curls. Then back beneath the surface.

As she followed it, it popped up again, this time giving her a nibble before sinking back beneath the surface of the placid, peaceful pond in the center of the perfect garden.

Cute, she thought.

He disappeared.

She flicked at the water to get his attention.

When the ripples settled, she saw him again, waiting just beneath the surface. She looked down at the fish, into his eyes, and the fish looked back at her.

His happy face was gone.

Instinctively, Suzze bolted upright as the fish jumped half her height, stopping even with her crotch, flapping his tail like a salmon swimming upstream, trying to fly that last few inches to take a bite, or so it seemed, before falling back into the pond and swimming around in circles, his dorsal fin breaking the surface like a shark planning his next attack.

"Shit!" Suzze dropped the hem of her robe and slid, slid, slid back to the bank, fast as she could go.

She stood on the bank, trying to focus underneath the surface to see if what she thought had happened, really did.

With no sign of the predator, she turned and walked back toward the Old Man.

"On the other hand, Jack, what Epicurious could have meant…"

"*Curus*. Epi-*curus*. Not Epi-*curious*." The Old Man couldn't stand it any longer.

"Yeah, whatever. What I think Epi-whoever meant was that we all get a choice. We can have any god we want. As long as we choose bad gods, we'll live with the consequences. The Jews. The Christians. The Muslims. They've had thousands of years to get it right and look where it got us."

Suzze stopped and squatted, rubbing and rocking on her heels to wipe her behind in the grass.

"What did their gods ever do for them? It's time for them to give it up. Get with the plan. Move on. I think they're willing. They just don't know how. They need to have faith in themselves."

Suzze walked over and nudged the Old Man with her foot. "Let's go someplace else."

Suzze and the Old Man walked up the hill.

"Where we headed, Jack?"

"Ever been to Washington?"

"Didn't really care for it. Too many people looking for a handout."

"Got somebody you need to meet," said the Old Man.

As they rounded the top of the hill, Suzze could see the Washington Monument in the distance.

"That fish back there, Jack. I swear he had fire in his eyes."

"Maybe he just wanted a piece of the devil."

"Or a piece of my ass," said Suzze.

- - -

The Indian Council of Medical Research (ICMR) released findings of a controversial study conducted by Dr. Dhruv Bangloveshi which examined the neural basis of religious and non-religious belief using Functional Magnetic Resonance Imaging (fMRI) and concluded that fewer than 9% of Christians were sincere in their belief. (Deemed "True Believers")

Two groups, one self-proclaimed "committed Christians," the other, self-identified "atheists, nonbelievers and freethinkers" were scanned as they evaluated the truth and falsity of religious and nonreligious propositions.

The research established that for both groups, statements of belief were associated with increased activation of the ventromedial prefrontal cortex, a region of the brain involved in emotional judgment, processing uncertainty, assessing rewards and thinking about oneself. A comparison of all religious trials to all nonreligious trials produced a wide range of signal differences throughout the brain and the processing of religious belief and empirical belief differed in significant ways. The regions associated with increased activation in response to religious stimuli included the anterior insula, the ventral striatum, the anterior cingulate cortex, and the posterior medial cortex.

It has long been held that Christianity is merely a meme, defined as an element of a culture or system of behavior that may be considered to be passed from one individual to another by nongenetic means, especially imitation of peers, or parental pressure -- commonly called "brainwashing."

The study, funded by Tatas, a multinational conglomerate headquartered in Uttar Pradesh and eager to enter the U.S. health insurance market, raised the question: Should health insurance pay for religious deprogramming which is estimated to cost billions?

Asked to summarize his findings in layperson's terms, Dr. Bangloveshi replied, "Just because Christians *believe* what they *want* to be true, doesn't mean that they believe it is *actually the truth*. To Christians, belief and reality are interchangeable and, although they may actually know the difference, as 91% of them do, to them it doesn't really matter."

I

Behind the Scenes with Connie and Cherry

So, start at the beginning. Why a book?
Why a book about a down and out televangelist?

(Connie)

I was sick and broke and lonely and had no friends, except for my bunnies, and my mother had died so I decided to write a book. I saved my extra money and once a month I bought a book about how to write a book. And I did. It was a painfully hard thing to do, much harder than I ever imagined it would be, but I did it. I finished it, saw it through to the very end. And then, of course, no one would publish it. So then, I bought another book and read blogs and learned how to do that myself, and now I'm here.

Was it worth it?

(Connie)

Financially? I don't know. With all the time and effort it takes, you'd have to make a million bucks to make it worth it if that's what you mean. But did it feel good to finish? To get out what's inside? Oh yes, that's what Suzze is all about. Whatever you're stuck with, get rid of it and move on. That's what I'm trying to do. Plus, I got to meet Cherry. I would never have met her if it weren't for Suzze.

Since you mentioned it, what is Suzze really about?

(Connie)

Suzze is about the Christian ideology of original sin clothed in the Freudian scatological subconscious. That's what somebody told me. I have no idea what it means. Suzze is about the power of belief and the horrible cost of ignorance, how, in an irrational society, it is ignorance that guides us and defines who we are, usually to a bad end.

Is there a lesson?

(Connie)

A lesson? Like a moral to the story? Well, I guess. There's always a moral. But I hope it's just a fun story. But I understand. Critics need something to latch on to, something to criticize I suppose or they wouldn't have a job, would they? They need to tell you how your fun story isn't literature, and Suzze isn't, literature, heaven forbid. So maybe the theme, or the lesson or the moral is that, as a country, America just needs to take a big, cleansing poop. There, I said it.

Where did it come from? Suzze and her Irritable Bowel Syndrome? Do you remember?

(Connie)

Yes I do. Like it was yesterday. I was watching Oprah and Dr. Oz came on, maybe the first time he was on TV. And he was playing in poop. And he just reminded me of a witch doctor, such a fraud, such a showman. But it occurred to me that if Oprah was pooping, then soon everybody would be pooping, they call that a meme, I think, when an idea catches on, when something that used to be not okay in public now is okay because somebody famous does it, and I said to myself, the world needs a story about a woman who poops.

How about the material? And the characters?
It's all Near Future.

(Connie)

I did not so much write Suzze as transcribe it. It was revealed to me. It was divinely inspired. I watched Jon Stewart. And Colbert. And the new guy, John Oliver, but most of all, Bill Maher. He wrote it. Spiritually. I was merely the vessel through which he flowed. I wanted to write Suzze as if it were played out on multiple segments of Stewart, or Maher, or Colbert. No doubt I have fallen far short, but, for better or worse, Suzze is my homage to them. As for the characters, what is really great about writing fiction is that I don't make up these people, these characters. I am them. Like an actor in a role. I act out the role and then sit down and record it. Sometimes it's just not there. But when it is, it's the most fun job in the world.

Who's your favorite? Which character?

(Connie)

Well, Suzze of course. But after that, it's the HushPuppies. [The HushPuppies debut late in Episode 3, CM] They're so much fun, fun to talk to, fun to listen to. They have no agenda. They're just along for the ride, to see where life takes them.

Is there any of Suzze in you?
Did you draw from your life experiences to create her?

(Connie)

That's a hard question to answer. We've never had the same life experiences, not even close. She and I are completely different in that respect. But I think we're both a little eccentric, a little ditsy. At least I've been told that. Now that I think about it, when I was a young woman and those things mattered, I was told by a man, an older man, he told me, he said, This is what you're good at, obvious trivialities. Obvious trivialities well spoken, he called them. I think that was just his way of saying BS. Well, I never knew if he meant it as a compliment or not and I was too embarrassed to ask and I never took it well but it always hung in my mind. And then one day I realized that whether he meant it to be a compliment or not, it was definitely true. And so, they say to do what you're good at. And I am good at that, obvious trivialities well spoken. Always have been. I was a smart-assed child. So I thought, be a smart ass. Do what you're good at. And that's Suzze. And I love her. And I love me for loving her.

You said you modeled Pastor Steve after Steven Colbert?

(Connie)

The master and his spawn. I watch Steven Colbert and about one show out of five I realize I've seen genius. He's like the biggest thing on TV and he's still underrated. And it has come to the point that you can't tell if he's still acting the part, or if he's living the part. I think that's it. Colbert the person has become Colbert the role. I think he's going to do something Michael Jackson-ish. Can't help it. He'll explode. So imagine what it would be like if a Christian psychopath modeled himself after Steven Colbert. The outcome would be just horrible.

(Cherry)

That's such bullshit. We went to see Steve Furtick. [*Elevation Church, Charlotte, NC*] He's the best show ever. The guy delivers. He's like the slickest little weasel you can imagine. And hot, hot, hot. He's like the opposite of George Clooney. All the guys want to f*** him and all the gals want to be his friend.

(Connie)

But Steven Colbert came first.

(Cherry)

Okay, I'll give you that. Now that I think about it, maybe Pastor Steve modeled himself after Pastor Colbert and from that came Pastor Steve in the book. They're all a little creepy if you ask me.

Was there a time when you wanted to quit and couldn't go on?

(Connie)

Oh sure. And at that exact moment, Dean Koontz spoke to me. I was reading one of his books, Odd Thomas, I think, and it's a book about a writer of popular fiction and he's giving advice. And this writer, this fictional writer in a Dean Koontz book is writing about a detective who has bulimia. Bulimia! Do you believe that? Dean Koontz stole my idea! And the problem I was having with Suzze was, I was trying to make her too high brow, too esoteric. I was trying to write satire or literature. I wanted to be Gore Vidal, the greatest writer of all time, I think, by the way, but I was just getting stuck, always trying to go higher and higher, to write better and better. And then I read what the author in the Koontz book, who, of course, is really Koontz himself playing Dean Koontz in the book, and who is more downmarket than Koontz?, and he said, and I remember this so I can almost quote it, Give the narrative a lighter tone than you think it deserves, dear boy, lighter than you think you can bear to give it, because you won't find the truth of life in morbidity, only hope. So Dean Koontz got me over the hump. And Dean Koontz is a genius.

Cherry, you've criticized Richard Dawkins, saying he's a bad preacher. What do you mean?

(Cherry)
Richard Dawkins seems to think that science, rational science maybe he would call it, can transform or convert religious people, who are not rational, with a rational argument. That is rare to the extreme. Essentially, it can't be done. As someone said, you can't reason someone out of something that they didn't reason themselves into in the first place. I agree with Dawkins that fundamentalist religion, if not all Yahweh-based religion, is a threat to mankind. But, unlike Dawkins, I think the best way to change, to convert a religious person, is to simply look them in the eye and say, You're an idiot, and walk away. Shame is the only argument they understand. Sad but true. Take a look at Maury or Jerry Springer. You look at those shows and think that they're reprehensible. But they're real. They're the real reality. At their core, they constantly shame and ridicule. And I think it works. Sad. Pitiful perhaps. But true.

Which church do you attend?

(Connie)
Do you mean which building do I go to? I don't. I spend Sundays reflecting, as I do every day.

(Cherry)

I like Elevation, the best show on earth. Pastor Steve? He's the man. I'd do him in the dirt.

Who would you most like to go to bed with?

(Connie)

What an inappropriate question! I don't have to go to bed. I rarely get out of bed. If you're talking romantically, well, that ship has sailed. But who do I find spectacularly attractive? Dinner and conversation and see what happens? If that's what you mean, I don't even have to think about it. Judy Woodruff.

The PBS newscaster?

Yep. My kind of woman.

May I ask if you have any digestive problems?

(Connie)

No. Never have. None whatsoever.

(Cherry)

Religious types make me want to puke. Does that count?

Interviewed by Chloë Martindale

About the Authors

Connie Wellborne, a retired librarian, lives in a blue house trailer behind Leonard's Garage in Gold Hill, North Carolina with, depending on the season, from one to ten dozen rabbits. 'Move Over Jesus' is her second novel.

Cherry Santana, as fate would have it, is also a librarian, downsized after seven years of loyal service, only to be rehired, part-time, with no benefits. She is now a librarian with a vengeance, all too prone to make it clear that she really doesn't give a damned if you read 'Fifty Shades of Gray' or not, and has no idea whatsoever if God will punish you if you do -- the question she is most often asked. (But he probably will.) (Let's hope so.)

Want more ?

Want it free?

Go to:
SuzzeOsmond.com/Book
to receive future episodes free.
No spam. No ads. No hassles.

And, oh yeah,
Reviews are Sacred!
Go to:
SuzzeOsmond.com/Reviews
to post comments, questions and reviews.

Stay tuned for Episode 3.

And always,
Be Nice.

www.SuzzeOsmond.com